MANY
POiNts
of
Me

Caroline Gertler

MANY POINTS of ME

 Greenwillow Books

AN IMPRINT OF HARPERCOLLINS*PUBLISHERS*

Many Points of Me
Text copyright © 2021 by Caroline Gertler
Illustrations copyright © 2021 by Vesper Stamper

The text of this book is set in Directors Cut Pro.
Book design by Sylvie Le Floc'h

Library of Congress Control Number: 2020949360

ISBN 978-0-06-302700-8 (hardcover)

First Edition

21 22 23 24 25 PC/LSCH 10 9 8 7 6 5 4 3 2 1

Greenwillow Books

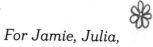

For Jamie, Julia,

and Elizabeth—my life;

and for my parents, where it began

MANY POINTS of ME

CHAPTER

one

Here's the thing about when your dad was a famous artist: he still lives. He still *is*. Because Mom is an art historian, I've always known that we talk about artists in the present tense. Even artists like Vermeer and Velazquez and Michelangelo, who died hundreds of years ago.

That's a good thing, and a bad thing. A good thing, because we still talk about Dad all the time. That's also why it's a bad thing: it's like we don't have to believe that he's actually gone.

And just like Dad still *is*, I'm beginning to think

that Theo Goodwin *was*. *Was* my best friend.

It's a cold, gray Sunday afternoon, late in January, and Theo and I are doing what we always do at the end of the weekend: drawing.

I'm sitting where I've sat a million times before, on the floor of Theo's room. Propped up in exactly the most comfortable position against the edge of his bed.

I know this room like the back of my hand. Where the wooden floorboards creak. Which threads hang loose in the navy blue rug. How to angle my knees to hold up my sketch pad.

Theo and I've been best friends all eleven years of our lives. We were born that way. Our moms have known each other since before they were pregnant with us—they're professors at the same college, we live in the same apartment building on the Upper West Side, and our birthdays are two days apart. Being best friends with Theo was hardly a choice.

I skim my pencil over the paper without looking

down to see what I'm making. It's called automatic drawing. The idea is to let your subconscious express itself.

Theo's drawing is the opposite of automatic. He sits in the swivel chair at his desk, hunched over his sketch pad in concentration. He's 100 percent focused as he tells the latest adventure of Theo-Dare. His comic book alter ego.

Where real Theo's hair color is rusty copper— also known as red—Theo-Dare's hair is mahogany. Real Theo wears wire-framed glasses and has a knack for peeling oranges in one piece. Theo-Dare has X-ray vision and can scale walls. Real Theo has a pet lizard; Theo-Dare has a trusty dragon sidekick. Real Theo gets sulky quiet when he's angry. Theo-Dare takes action.

Right now real Theo is speaking a mile a minute: "So then the alarm goes off, and security comes running. And you can't even believe how many security guards there are. They're everywhere. So Theo-Dare runs up to the roof, but there's nowhere to go. The gap between the buildings is too wide to jump."

Theo opens his arms to show me how wide.

"He's standing on the precipice, contemplating the fall to the pavement five stories below. And you're thinking, how's he going to get himself out of *this* situation?"

Theo turns back to his drawing. The swishing noise of the pencil gets stronger as he shades with the pencil edge. He tweaks some lines with his lucky eraser. It's lucky because it was a gift from me for our ninth birthdays. It's shaped like a paint palette, with little circles of color. I saw it at the gift shop at the Metropolitan Museum of Art and knew I had to get it for Theo. He's careful to use only one side to make it last as long as possible.

"Suddenly, a soft buzzing noise grows louder and louder. He swats at the air, thinking it's a mosquito. But it sounds more mechanical than that. He looks up. It's a bird, it's a plane . . . it's Super G!

Zooming in on her new stealth drone." Theo draws three strong pencil lines, emphasizing the drama.

Super G. That's me—Georgia. A few stories ago, Theo decided Theo-Dare couldn't go it alone. He needed a partner in crime. That's where Super G comes in.

Real Georgia is paper white with shoulder-length black hair. Super G has rosy, sharp cheeks and a flowing, glossy mane. Real Georgia tries to make herself disappear. Super G stands tall and proud, ready to take on the world.

Real Georgia is starting to wonder how she feels about her best friend.

Super G is loyal to a fault.

As Theo describes Super G hitching Theo-Dare to a harness and airlifting him with her drone, I look down at the automatic drawing on my sketch pad page.

It's nothing. Not even a flower, or hearts, or geometric shapes—the things I'd normally doodle in my notebooks during school. Just a mess of lines. A spiral that turns and turns in on itself until it's an angry tangle.

Ever since Dad died one year, nine months, and twenty-seven days ago, I haven't been able to draw. Not in the way I want to.

Sure, I can do a pretty good copy of an object if you set it in front of me. Like flowers in a vase, or a stack of books on a shelf. That's called figurative art—images that look like something in the real world.

The kind of art I *want* to make—the kind of art Dad made—is abstract. Art that shows feeling through form, color, and texture. Shapes that float on backgrounds of color, splatters and drips, lines made with a straight edge. *Direct expressions of feeling* is how Dad explained it. I *used* to think I knew what that meant.

"So that's cool, right, G?" Theo asks, swiveling away from his desk toward me.

I missed it. "You mean the drone?"

"Yeah, don't you like the idea of it being solar

powered? So in the story, it's nighttime and they're running low on energy?"

"Sure." I turn back to my paper, to see if my drawing can be made into anything more than a mess of spirals.

Because a mess of spirals is not what abstract art is about. Some people think that any little kid could make a Jackson Pollock painting—as simple as flinging paint onto a canvas. But a real artist knows it's not that easy. For one thing, it's about being the original person to come up with the idea and the technique. For another, it's about having a *feeling*. Something important that you want to share with the world. Like how Theo can lead a whole alternate life in his Theo-Dare comics.

"Just a sec." Theo jumps up from his chair. "Bathroom break."

I run through ideas of what I could turn my automatic drawing into: A squally ocean. A sinister forest. Or—it's late in the day and my stomach is rumbling with hunger—something sweet, like chocolate cake.

A birthday cake. Our twelfth birthdays are in less than a month. Theo and I have always celebrated together. On February twenty-first, the day between our birthdays. Our moms started the tradition of having a special dinner at home and a cake that we bake.

I glance at the photograph that Theo keeps on his bedside table. It's in a red frame with a sign in loopy blue cursive that says, "My First Birthday." A bunch of balloons in primary colors decorate the frame's corners. I wonder why Theo's mom framed that photograph for him and my mom didn't frame it for me.

In it, we're sitting side by side on the floor of my kitchen, birthday cakes before us, our chubby thighs and belly rolls spilling out of diapers. We're each reaching for the other one's cake, smashing into it. Chocolate frosting smeared everywhere.

I pick up the frame and study the picture more closely because something catches my eye: the toe of a boot in the corner. Not just any toe of any boot, but *Dad's* toe—the brown leather work boots he always wore. I've never noticed, because the brown leather blends in with the brown of the floor.

Now that I do notice, all I want is to keep that piece of Dad for myself.

I could ask for a copy of the photograph, but I don't just want my own copy—I also don't want Theo to have it. That tiny piece of Dad.

Theo already has more of Dad than I do: a drawing that Dad gave to him. Theo and I used to draw with Dad after school. Sometimes we'd play art games, like when Theo challenged Dad to draw a self-portrait in forty-five seconds. Dad did it, in this style that's between figurative and abstract. He doodled a bit on the back while Theo and I finished our drawings. And then later, before Theo went home for dinner, he handed it to Theo. "A gift for you," he'd said. My eyes narrowed as Theo pressed the paper to his chest like it was a map for buried treasure. Which it was, in a way.

Because even though Dad and I made art together all the time, and his drawings and sketches were scattered all over our apartment, and I could've kept any one of them for myself, it wasn't the same as him handing that drawing to Theo. *Choosing* to give it to him. He never made a drawing like that for me.

The one time I told Mom how jealous I was of Theo being so close to Dad, she said I needed to be more sympathetic. Theo never had a father—he bailed before Theo was born, leaving behind only Theo's red hair.

But right now, I don't feel any sympathy. Only jealousy, burning in my chest like I've just done the mile run in zero-degree weather.

I could steal the photograph, but Theo might realize it was missing. Or—

I grab a pair of scissors from Theo's desk.

My heart pounds as I slide the photograph from the frame, cut out the corner of the picture with Dad's toe in it, and put the photograph back.

I slip the corner into my pocket. Just that tiny piece.

That one piece of Dad.

The sole living thing that witnessed what I did is Krypto, Theo's pet bearded dragon. He's pressed against the glass of his tank, his neck puffed up. Theo says that's a sign of aggression in lizards.

"Sorry, Krypto." I turn to the tank, pretending I just got up from the floor to talk to him, as Theo's footsteps approach.

I won't apologize to Theo; he'll never know what's missing. Krypto won't tell him.

"Aw, isn't Krypto sweet?" Theo crouches down next to me. I can't see his eyes through the glare off his glasses, but I can picture his devoted expression. "Hey, little guy." He shifts the mesh cover and reaches in to give Krypto a few gentle strokes.

I don't get his fondness for Krypto. When Theo said he was getting a pet for his seventh birthday, I'd hoped for a pet with fur. A dog or a cat. Even a hamster or a guinea pig. But a visit to the doctor confirmed that Theo's allergic, and his mom has a thing about rodents, so it had to be a reptile. Which Theo was kind of psyched about, because it's more original than all those other pets anyway. And he named him Krypto, for Superman's dog, which we thought was so cool when we were seven.

The first time I held Krypto, his softness surprised me. He even seems to like me. Sometimes we play a game where we put him on the floor in the middle of Theo's room, and Krypto chooses *me* almost every single time. No idea why. It's not like I'm the one who feeds him. I can't even *watch* Theo feeding him—live crickets. The highlight of Theo's week.

Theo secures Krypto's tank cover and goes back to his desk chair. "So. Where were we?"

I've completely lost the thread, but I know Theo's testing to make sure I was paying attention. I make my best guess. "The drone, right?"

"You betcha." He returns to his drawing.

"Super G swoops in on her solar-powered stealth drone and saves the day."

If only Theo knew how far real Georgia is from saving the day.

It's almost the opposite: Theo's creating yet another brilliant comic book, and all I've got is a scribble on my sketch pad and the corner of a photograph in my pocket.

Theo never draws a messy tangle of spirals by accident. Even his doodles are like masterpieces.

Like my dad. Hank Rosenbloom, the great artist. Sometimes I wonder if Theo and I were accidentally switched at birth in the hospital. He's the child my dad should've had.

And that much becomes even clearer to me over dinner that night.

CHAPTER
two

The four of us sit in our usual seats at the long wooden table, open cartons of Chinese food dotted among us. Me and Mom, Theo and his mom, Harriet. We missed our usual pizza-and-movie Saturday night because Harriet had a date with the visiting professor in her economics department, so we're making it up with Chinese takeout Sunday night instead.

The table is in our living room, which doubled as Dad's studio. The walls, once covered with Dad's paintings, are mostly bare. His paintings are in storage. All that's left are hooks and wires where they used to hang. And the dried pools and drips of paint on the worn wooden table, which was Dad's drafting table. I trace the paint drips and study them for patterns; I count the colors to see which Dad used the most. Blues, blacks, browns, whites. A hidden message, maybe. But as much as I look for meaning, the paint drips are random.

Mom fills us in on the exhibition she's curating about Dad at the Met. It's scheduled to open in April, the two-year anniversary of his death.

Mom's job as an art history professor at Columbia keeps her super busy at all hours: preparing seminar notes, doing research, and marking papers and exams. And now she spends whatever free time she did have as the executor of Dad's estate. *Executor* means that Mom is in charge of Dad's art. She works with all sorts of art world people—museum curators, gallery owners, art dealers, and collectors. She sells paintings when we need money.

"We've settled on a title." She dabs a paper napkin at the brown sauce in the corner of her mouth. "*Hank Rosenbloom: Artist and Man.* You like that?"

I'm not sure if I do. It's a retrospective exhibition, which means it's a look back at Dad's career and his personal life. If it were up to me, it'd be called something like *Hank Rosenbloom: Dad Who I Miss More Than Anything.* But that wouldn't work for anyone else. So I sip my Sprite—a takeout-night treat—and keep quiet.

"Sounds cool," Theo says, accidentally spitting a grain of rice across the table toward my plate. I swipe it up with my napkin.

"Thanks." Mom smiles at Theo, not bothered, or even noticing, that *he* talks with food in his mouth. But if she catches one glimpse of me with my mouth open and a speck of food in there, I'd get a whole lecture on the dangers of choking.

"It'll be like a grand memorial service for Hank," Harriet says as she makes another moo-shu wrap.

"The next best thing to having him here with us."

Mom closes her eyes as if she's summoning Dad's presence to join us. If he *were* here, he'd be sitting in his usual chair at the head of the table, with the biggest, most overstuffed moo-shu wrap of us all. He'd mainly try to get shredded chicken bits, which worked for Mom, who prefers the vegetables. I always got to fill my wrap first so I could have an even mix of everything.

The truth is, there isn't a next-best thing to Dad being here. He can't be replaced with his art, even if that's what people do—especially Mom. It's like she throws herself into her work on Dad and the exhibit—doing research on paintings, deciding which ones to include, writing catalogue entries— so she can forget that he's actually gone.

Mom opens her eyes and looks straight at Theo. Not at me. *Him.*

"Theo, I've been meaning to ask you something. We're about to go to print with the exhibition catalogue, and we have a few spare pages. I was brainstorming ideas with Evelyn Capstone, the curator in charge. We thought it could be special to include a Q&A with you—you could tell the story in your own words about how you inspired Hank's asterism series."

I can't even believe what I'm hearing. Part of me thinks Mom can't be serious about including a Q&A with Theo Goodwin in the catalogue of *my* dad's exhibition.

What about a Q&A with me—about what it was like to be Hank's daughter? Isn't that more important than Theo's *claim* to be the inspiration for his greatest paintings?

Mom catches the expression on my face, because then she turns to me. "You, too, Georgia. You and Theo could do the Q&A together."

"Thanks, but no thanks." There's no way I'm going to play tagalong to Theo's moment of glory. Theo gives me a curious look.

"As you wish," Mom says. A joke between us— that she's the Westley to my Princess Buttercup from *The Princess Bride,* one of our favorite movies. It usually makes me crack a smile, but not tonight.

After dinner, they do what Mom calls "prep" for the Q&A. A conversation to discuss ideas that will go into the real thing, which has to be done next week, to make it into the catalogue in time. Mom and Theo and Harriet sit on the couch in the living room, Mom's phone between them to record their conversation.

I say I have homework and go to my room. But I leave my bedroom door cracked open, then tiptoe out to stand at the exact spot in the hallway where they can't see me and I can hear them. I settle in to listen, leaning my head and shoulder into the wall.

"Where should we start?" Mom asks in her Mom-teacher voice. A younger version of how she talks to her college students. The way she used to talk to me when she tried to help me with math in lower school. Before she laughed it off and said sixth-grade math was way too complicated for her. "Tell me what you remember."

Without even seeing Theo's face, I know he's giving his saintly look: his mouth wide, the glimmer in his eyes, the glow of his skin beneath his copper freckles. The look that shows his pure goodness as a person, how he's always there for me. The look that, lately, makes me feel guilty, somehow. Of what, I don't know.

"It was dark early that night, so it must've been winter," Theo begins. I only heard him tell this story once, at the shiva after Dad's funeral, and that was more than enough times for me. But now it sounds like a story he's told, either out loud or to himself, a thousand times before. "It was just Georgia and me, and Hank, and it was dark enough for us to see stars through his telescope."

Hearing Theo tell it brings me back to those nights. Dad's biggest passion, aside from art, was astronomy. Studying the stars through his telescope on our balcony. He'd let us join him sometimes.

Dad called Theo and me his binary stars: two stars that orbit around the same center and appear from Earth to be a single point of light.

"And what did you ask him that night?" Mom prompts.

Theo continues, "I asked him, 'Have you ever tried to paint the stars?'"

It hurts in my chest, hearing him repeat it now, a question that's echoed in my head countless times since he first asked it.

Immediately I wished *I'd* been the one who'd asked. Because Dad did that thing he did when someone said something that was important and interesting and really made him think: he got all quiet. He put his fingers to his lips and thumb on his chin and didn't say a word.

Other people might feel the need to speak, to answer your question right away. Not Dad. He knew it was okay to take his time, to find the right words. It made me sparkle inside, the times I said something that Dad reacted to that way. More often, it was Theo who said those kinds of things.

"After a long pause, Dad—I mean Hank—said, 'Not yet, Theo. But I will.'"

Wait—did Theo just call him *Dad*? Sometimes he did that, by mistake. Because I always called him *Dad*, of course. And all he ever knew was my dad. Until we both lost him.

But hearing Theo call him *Dad* now, even by accident, rankles me in a way it never did when Dad was here. *I'm* the only person who has the right to call him that. He was *my* dad. Not Theo's.

I want to go out there and yell at them all, to tell them Theo wasn't that important to Dad. I was. But that's not the truth. We all know it.

The anger in my belly moves down into my feet, and I'm walking into the room before I can stop myself.

Just as Mom says, "And he did, didn't he, Theo? He painted the stars?"

Tears of joy spring to Theo's eyes as he nods yes. Actual tears. He swipes at them beneath his

MaNY POiNts of Me

glasses. Harriet grabs his hand in hers.

I can't stand to watch anymore. I run back to my room before they look up and see me.

I don't need to hear Theo retelling the rest of the story. I know it. I lived it—I was there when Dad made those paintings.

Dad didn't paint the actual stars. Copying constellations wasn't what interested him. Instead, he made up his own groups of stars: asterisms.

Asterisms are patterns of stars that people recognize, like the Big Dipper, but that aren't official, like constellations. Most people think the Big Dipper is a constellation, but it's actually an asterism that's part of the constellation Ursa Major, the big bear.

Dad brought home giant canvases as big as windows, which made you feel like you were immersed in the galaxy. First he primed them in white. Then our house filled with buckets and buckets of black paint. Different types of black: bone black, carbon black, lamp black, roman black.

Those cans of paint are still lined up on the wooden trestles Dad used to store his paints. Along with cans of every other color he used. They're probably dried up and evaporated by now, but Mom doesn't have the heart to throw them out.

He laid the canvases on the floor, and he poured the paint directly from the buckets. Thicker and thicker and thicker onto the canvas, until it dried in crusts and waves and pools. Mixing those black paints to form his own unique background.

And then he dug into the thick background with stippling tools, to create wells for the glowy-white mixture of paint he used to make the stars.

He invented his own asterisms. Three of them.

First *Bird in the Tree*, inspired by the birds of Central Park, which he'd studied for an earlier series he'd made. Then *Sally in the Stars*, for Mom. And third, *Man on the Moon*, his self-portrait.

They're powerful and majestic, and everyone said the asterism series was going to be his breakout work. The work that would launch him into being one of the greats. Whatever that meant. He said that he wanted the series to hang together in its own room or gallery space, like the Rothko Chapel.

But he couldn't keep them together—we needed the money to live, Mom explains, and each of the three paintings sold for a lot of money: *Bird in the Tree* to a private collector, *Sally in the Stars* to the Met, and *Man on the Moon* to the Whitney Museum. I don't know for how much, but enough that Mom and Dad would giggle at night about how they didn't have to worry about bills and expenses the same way anymore. Mom said he should make a hundred asterisms, so she'd never have to work again. But Dad said four was a good number for a series. One more and he'd be done.

Dad primed the canvas for the fourth asterism. But then he got sick and was gone before he could paint it, and that plain white unfinished canvas still sits in the corner by his paint trestles, where he'd left it to dry.

Blank—a big empty question mark.

The day Dad died, Mom held me close and whispered things in my ear, between sobs, about how much he loved me. She said Dad told her that he'd planned for his last asterism to be of me.

But there's no real proof of what Dad planned. Nothing on paper.

Mom says the asterisms came pretty much fully formed to Dad. He worked out some details for the first three on random scraps of paper as he painted. But he didn't make any actual studies for them, like he did for his Bird series. So there aren't any sketches for the last asterism to show what he was planning to do.

Maybe what he told Mom was just an idea. Maybe he would've changed his mind. Maybe he never really said that and she made it up, to try to make me feel better. Because he left nothing—nothing that can be put on display in the Met and written up in the catalogue to show that he meant to paint me.

At first, after the funeral and shiva and all,

Mom turned that unfinished canvas to face the wall. She said she couldn't stand it looking at us. But we both thought it was worse seeing the back— the wooden frame, the staples tacking the canvas to the stretcher. So Mom turned it to face us again.

Eventually *she* decided that there's something nice about wondering exactly how the last asterism painting would've looked, like there's still an open conversation we can have with Dad in our heads about it. But for me, it's just a reminder of the emptiness. Like a tombstone.

As the months—and then a year, and more months—passed, the canvas became kind of invisible. It faded into the background, becoming a part of the white wall behind it.

Until now.

Until Theo tells that story about how he inspired Dad.

Which makes my throat tight and my eyes burn, and I bite the inside of my cheek to keep myself from crying. I wish Dad had wanted to make an asterism of me. But without any proof—I won't let myself believe it. Sometimes Theo and I talk about it, and he's sure it would've been me, to complete the family.

But who's to say it wouldn't have been Theo?

Though I'd never say that out loud to Theo. I don't want him to think he might've been that special to Dad. That important. Even if he was.

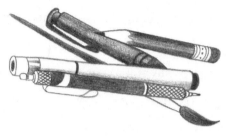

CHAPTER
three

Sometimes, people change. Or the way you feel about someone or something changes. It could be lots of little things that make your feelings change. Or one big thing. Or a combination of both. That's how it is with me and art.

In school the next day, Monday, there's a flyer printed on green paper, stapled to the bulletin board at the entrance to Mr. Butterweit's art studio. The announcement of the annual NYC ART competition. Now that we're in sixth grade, we finally get to enter, and I'm supposed to be excited.

Instead, I feel like I've swallowed a rusty anchor.

NYC ART is a super-important citywide art competition for sixth through twelfth graders. Ten winners from each grade get their entries displayed in an exhibit at the Metropolitan Museum of Art in the spring—this year, the same time as the opening of the Hank Rosenbloom exhibition. And they win a one-thousand-dollar award to use for art classes or supplies.

No one's more determined to get into NYC ART than Theo. He wants to go to Evergreen, a specialized arts high school, for ninth grade, and he thinks that if he gets into NYC ART three years in a row, it'll make his application an ace. Not to mention that he's been keeping a list of what he could do with that thousand-dollar award. His mom doesn't have a lot of extra money for art. He relies on me to share my endless supplies.

"Self-portrait, that's a good one." Theo reads the theme of this year's competition over my shoulder. I catch a whiff of pretzels and hummus on his breath, and that, combined with the glow of copper—the color I'd use to paint Theo—jars with the minty green of the NYC ART flyer. My stomach clenches with queasiness. I used to want nothing more than to get into NYC ART, but now I'm not so sure.

"Self-portrait, ugh." I've been making self-portraits since I first learned to draw a stick figure at the age of two. It's only the most common art-class assignment ever. But now that it counts for something—a competition—making a self-portrait seems like the worst possible idea.

"C'mon, self-portrait is so easy," Theo scoffs, flicking his head to sweep the rusty hair out of his eyes.

"I was hoping for still life." Copying a bunch of objects on a table—that'd be easy. In French they call it *nature morte,* which literally means nature dead. The whole point of a still life is that it doesn't move. It doesn't change. It just is. Unlike people, who never seem to stay the same.

I take a deep breath as we read through the competition guidelines:

❏ *All submissions must be original work.*

❏ *Entries must be submitted by a teacher—maximum four entries per grade.*

❏ *There may be more than one winner per school, but no more than two per grade level.*

❏ *All media are acceptable, and creative use of materials is encouraged.*

"We've got this, G. We're in it together, right? Team Theo-Dare–Super G!" Theo puts out his hands for a double fist-bump secret handshake, but other girls are filing past us now—Harper Willis, Violet Avilez, and Chloe Chen—and I pretend I don't notice.

I inhale the smells as we walk into the art studio—the mix of oil with pine and clay and charcoal. Smells that offer comfort in their familiarity, and worry. Worry that I'll never make the kind of art everyone expects of me. The kind of art Theo can make, that Dad made.

Mr. Butterweit looks up from the papers he's flipping through at his large metal desk at the front of the room. "NYC ART!" he says to us. "You two ready to begin? The countdown is on."

Entries are due in two weeks.

Theo gives a thumbs-up. I roll my eyes. I'm not sure I want to begin. *Can* begin.

Other kids ripple around us, dropping their backpacks and taking their places at the stools along both sides of the drafting tables.

Mr. Butterweit's made it clear from the beginning of the year that Theo and I are the best artists in sixth grade and should be aiming to get into NYC ART. Theo because, no question, he's the best. And me, because, yes, I *do* have skill. Or *did*. But mostly—I bet—because of who my dad was.

Mr. Butterweit's eyes popped out of their sockets on the first day of art when I confirmed that I am Georgia Rosenbloom, daughter of *the* Hank Rosenbloom.

"I *love* Hank Rosenbloom. *Adore* his work," Mr.

Butterweit said, rubbing his hands together like he couldn't wait to get a piece of Hank Rosenbloom.

I gave back the tight smile I'd learned to give to people saying things like that. First, it shows how weird things get when people talk about artists in the present tense, like Dad still *is*. Even when he *isn't*. Second, someone like Mr. B thinks of Dad as his art, as a product, like a beautiful thing you can buy in a store.

But he was my *dad*. He sang me "Moonshadow" at bedtime and "Morning Has Broken" to wake me up, taught me to ride a bike, flipped blueberry pancakes for weekend breakfasts, and hugged me tight in his arms whenever we said goodbye.

Except for the last time. Because he couldn't.

I swallow down that thought, biting the sore on the inside of my cheek that's come from so many months of holding in tears.

Theo and I go to our seats at the drafting table. He sits on the window side, all the way at the head of the table, as close to Mr. B's desk as possible.

I sit a few seats down, diagonal from him, on the side facing the windows. I like to look up and stare outside when I'm thinking. Theo doesn't need to look anywhere but at his own work.

I'm relieved to get away from Theo and his copper color and hummus breath and hair flicking. And his concern for me. When he's not trying to be funny and saying things like "Georgia, reenter the orbit," and telling me about the latest adventures of Theo-Dare and Super G, he's asking me if I'm okay.

I'm tired of it.

And I like that the new girl, Harper Willis, chooses to sit next to me. That we're becoming friends.

Today there are handheld mirrors at everyone's places in addition to the usual drawing paper and baskets of sharpened pencils and gummy erasers. The unexpectedness of the mirrors creates a wave of chatter and giggles. The noise rises to a roar in the room as kids make funny faces at themselves.

"Quiet down, class! We're going to start our

study of self-portraits today," Mr. B says as the voices fall to a hush. "The NYC ART competition theme has just been announced, and while only a few of you will enter, we'll all be working toward completing self-portraits. So let's start by taking a look at yourselves."

"Your hair is getting longer," Harper whispers, holding up her mirror, distracting me.

My almost-black hair has always been chin length, with bangs cut straight across, just above my eyebrows. I never cared much one way or another until Harper started telling me I should grow it long. "It's your best feature," she says.

Now my hair falls to my shoulders, and I like how I can see it out of the corner of my eyes when I turn my head to look in the mirror. I like how growing out my bangs and tucking them behind my ears or clipping them to the side means that my green eyes pop like sea glass. Like something Harper would've found on the beach where she grew up.

Most of the kids at our school have been together since kindergarten, but Harper's family moved here this year from California. Right away everyone noticed her. It was hard not to. Especially because she came after the school year started, just before Halloween.

There'd been five days of rain and wind, bringing a heavy gloom to the city. When it cleared, Harper arrived. She was all brightness and light with her golden-brown skin and long, curly brown hair that looks like it's never been cut. It falls past her waist. And it isn't just one shade of brown. Sun bleached, it has so many colors in it, from oak to bronze to ash.

When I first met Harper, I was certain that the color I'd pick to paint her would be marigold. Bright and sunny. It was like Harper brought the sun with her.

I knew who she'd become friends with, and it wasn't me and Theo. She'd fit right in with Violet Avilez and Chloe Chen, the prettiest girls in our grade. The girls who get the starring roles in the school plays, with their shiny hair, eyeliner, and quick way with words. They made a seat for her at their table in the cafeteria and got her a mermaid costume to match theirs for the middle school Halloween party in the gym. Chloe was the pink mermaid; Violet was purple. But I liked Harper's mermaid best: aqua. Not the marigold I would've chosen, but once I saw her as aqua, I realized almost any color could work for her. Her colors keep changing.

Theo and I dressed as artists, which was kind of pointless because everyone already thinks of us as artists. We were Theo and Vincent van Gogh. He was Theo, of course, and I was Vincent, with a bandage taped over my right ear. Theo was so proud that he found the perfect blue hat lined in black faux fur to order on the Internet and a green overcoat of his mom's that I could borrow to wear, so I looked just like the real thing. I carried a paint palette and Theo held a blank canvas, and we'd form these vignettes around the room where I'd actually paint on the canvas that he held up for me.

It was all kind of fun until the Mermaids noticed us, and I saw the look on Violet's and Chloe's faces. And I suddenly felt like a total weirdo dressed as a man who'd chopped off his own ear. For the first time, I cared what those girls thought. I ran to the bathroom and pretended to Theo that I'd gotten sick and had to go home.

Theo walked home with me and offered to bring some toast or saltines from his apartment since our moms had gone to a faculty party. I said he'd better keep his distance because I didn't want to get him sick. But the fact is, I didn't want to end up telling Theo the truth. I didn't want to hurt his feelings because *he* wasn't embarrassed by our costumes. I gave him back his mom's coat, but he insisted that I keep the blue hat, to remember how great our costumes were. I stuffed it on a top shelf of my bookcase because I didn't want to remember, but every once in a while I get a glimpse of it, and I feel that embarrassment all over again.

Now I tune back in to Mr. B asking us what we think it means to make a self-portrait. "Why would an artist be compelled to draw or paint their own image?"

Luca Banks raises his hand, bouncing off his stool. "Because he thinks he's the best-looking guy he knows!"

Everyone laughs. Even Mr. B chuckles.

"Faces are hard," Chloe calls out. "Maybe they like the challenge?"

"That's true," Mr. B says. "Faces are challenging to draw, which is why we're going to break it down into forms and general proportions, looking at features as units. For example, eyes are generally in the middle of the face, centered between the chin and the top of the head, and most faces are five eyes wide. But not every face is perfectly symmetrical—far from it—and there are artists who break those rules, too."

He flashes through a series of self-portraits by Pablo Picasso, starting when he was a teenager and drew himself naturalistic, to his twenties, when he starts to make himself look exaggerated and sculptural. And then, in his fifties, with a drawing where both his eyes are on one side of his head and nothing is symmetrical or in proportion.

"Why would Picasso choose to paint himself this way?" Mr. B asks.

Theo raises his hand. "He's exploring new ways to express the same idea."

"Yes, Theo. And what is that idea?" I feel like Mr. B is looking directly at me, like I should know the answer.

And I do. Self-portrait is about making a visual representation of yourself. Sometimes you need to skew things on the outside in order to show how shattered you feel inside. But that thought makes me feel panicky. So I pretend to look down at my paper, and let Mr. B call on Alex Cohen.

"The idea of knowing who you are?" Alex says like it's a question, not a statement.

"Exactly." Mr. B nods. He starts flashing images of other famous artists' self-portraits: Rembrandt, Chuck Close, Frida Kahlo, and van Gogh (thankfully the one of him in a straw hat at the Met, not the one that we modeled my Halloween costume on). "The best portraits go beneath the surface to capture a sense of who the person is, or was. They reveal the truth of an artist. Truth with a capital *T*. That's the idea—Truth—that I want us all to explore through our self-portraits. We'll begin by sketching in pencil—the most direct way to get feelings on paper."

Maybe that's why self-portraits make me nervous. Because it means finding my Truth. Who I really am. And if an artist like van Gogh will go so far as to chop off his own ear to figure it out, maybe I don't really want to know, anyway.

Harper probably never questions who she really is. She's making fish faces at me and doodling on my paper. A stick-figure cartoon of Mr. B looking at himself in the mirror and patting his belly. I let out a snort of laughter.

Theo's eyes bore into me, watching from his seat down the table. His hair sticks up like a halo, lit by the window behind him. Like he's an angel, judging me from above. Theo knows his Truth. He is a true artist. Maybe that's why he inspired Dad to paint the stars, and I didn't.

I make a Harper-style fish face at him, but he doesn't smile. His eyes dart back to his own mirror, and he keeps them glued there, as if he can find the answer to the world's problems in his own reflection, on his own paper.

My mirror shows me nothing. It reveals no Truth, that's for sure.

For the rest of class, I try to relax into making an easy sketch of myself. But my hand is stiff, and I grip the pencil so tightly that my palm gets sweaty and clammy. I'm far from smooth like I used to be when I drew with Dad at home, in our studio.

When Mr. B announces it's time to wrap up, my drawing hardly even looks like a face that a five-year-old would make. The eyes are just ovals, the nose a right angle. Nothing that I can use for a self-portrait.

I crumple it up and toss it in the trash.

CHAPTER
four

After class Harper links her arm in mine and pulls me along to the door. But I always wait for Theo after art. It takes him a few minutes to come back to reality after he's been in his drawing zone.

"I just have to . . . um . . . wait for a sec." I stall for time, pretending to study the rules on the NYC ART flyer. Lunch is next, and Harper sits at the cool kids' table with Chloe and Violet. I always sit with Theo and the musical theater kids. It doesn't make sense for me to walk off to the cafeteria with Harper, without Theo.

"No probs." Harper swings her hair over her shoulder and starts braiding it in her fidgety way. As she twists and coils the strands, the different colors of her hair swirl together. Her marigold color is looking more orange today. Neon orange, like a flashing sign, signaling for me to follow.

Theo stands up front, chatting with Mr. Butterweit. When he sees me dawdling, he gives a quick wave and runs over, like an eager puppy, which I used to find reassuring, but now just makes me think I shouldn't have waited. If I'd left with Harper, maybe I could've tried sitting at her table. Just for once.

"Lunch?" he asks. I nod.

Harper relinks her arm in mine as we head down the hall to the cafeteria.

Theo walks on my other side. I could link arms with him, too, but his copper color, which never changes, doesn't go with Harper's neon orange.

"What are you thinking for your portrait?" he asks me, ignoring Harper.

"I don't know." I'm not thinking anything. "I'm

probably just going to make mine straightforward. More of a Rembrandt than a Picasso."

"What, you mean you don't want to paint yourself with two eyes on one side of your head?" Harper says.

Theo ignores her. "G, you're going to have to focus if you want to be competitive."

Competitive grates like nails on a chalkboard to my ears.

I give my new, longer hair a little flip. "I just feel like—I have too much else going on right now."

"Like what? What could be more important than this?"

"How could you forget," Harper pipes up. "*Someone* has a big birthday. Twelve!"

"So do I," Theo says. "My birthday is two days after hers."

"It is?" Harper looks at me like she's wondering why I didn't share that piece of information. I didn't think she'd care that Theo's birthday is practically the same day as mine.

"But so what," Theo continues. "It doesn't take three weeks to plan your birthday. It *could* take three months to make a self-portrait good enough to submit. And we don't have three months. We only have two weeks!"

"Twelve's a big birthday!" I don't know where these words are coming from. It's like I'm channeling Harper—the kind of thing she would say.

"We're working on ideas," Harper says.

We are? I look at her and she smiles. And just like that, her color shifts, from neon orange to softer, warmer marigold again.

"Aren't we going to do our usual?" There's a note of panic in Theo's voice.

I want to say yes to him, like always. But then I remember his tears of joy at Mom asking him to do the Q&A. "Maybe I also want something different."

"Yeah, Georgia told me she never does anything special for her birthday. I'm making it my mission to get this girl to have some fun for once!"

I cringe at Harper's words. I know she doesn't

realize how they're hurting Theo, that I described our usual as nothing special.

Theo's face drops. For a moment I feel his heart like my own. I get a pang of guilt for removing that piece of Dad from his photograph yesterday.

I think fast how to fix it, though Theo can see right through me. "I didn't mean it's not *special*. I just meant that I—we—always do something at home."

"So, Theo, why don't you come, too?" Harper asks, like it'd be the most natural thing in the world.

Really? But I say what I think Harper would want to hear: "Yeah. It'll be fun."

I try to picture what Harper might plan: me, Theo, and Harper going out to a Japanese restaurant, ordering sushi platters, even though I only eat avocado and cucumber rolls. I bet Harper is a sushi expert.

"Chloe and Violet can make it!" Harper announces.

That's where my vision falls apart. Theo and I have *never* been close with Chloe and Violet.

There was a time that Chloe and I had a bunch of playdates when we were in the same class in first and second grades. But then in fourth grade she was one of the first girls to get a phone, and she started taking voice lessons and going to concerts, and we were never in the same homeroom again.

I sense Theo pulling away; he won't have a place at that kind of party. I'm not sure I will, either.

"And something else big." Harper nudges my side with her elbow.

"Oh, right." I haven't told Theo yet, and now doesn't seem like the time. If I keep my expression flat, maybe he won't push. But he's not like that.

"What?" Theo asks. "What else?"

"Hasn't Georgia told you?" Harper raises her eyebrows.

"Told me what?"

"Nothing, it's not a big deal," I protest.

"It's a huge deal!" Harper bursts out. At this moment I wish she wasn't so enthusiastic about every little thing. "Georgia agreed to design

Valentine's Day cards for us. We're selling them to raise money for charity."

Harper asked me about it last week. She said the Mermaids were raising money for a shelter for homeless women and children, and they wanted me to come up with designs for Valentine's Day cards to sell. At first I couldn't believe she was asking *me*, who never gets asked to participate in anything by anybody. But Valentine's Day isn't really my thing, so I said I wasn't sure. Then Harper pulled me into a lavender-and-jasmine–scented hug and said I had to, that I was the one-and-only artist who could do it. So I said yes.

"Wow, that's gonna take a lot of time," Theo says. "No way you can do card designs and enter NYC ART."

"I haven't done anything yet!"

Harper wags her finger at me. "You promised. Remember the first planning meeting—my house after school on Friday." Harper's house. Her parents are big art collectors. She thought it was so cool when she met me that Hank Rosenbloom's my dad, because her parents own one of his paintings, and I'll get to see it when I go to her house.

"Yes, yes," I say, leading the way into the syrup-scented cafeteria. Breakfast-for-lunch day.

Harper tugs me toward the table where Chloe and Violet sit. It's full, except for two chairs crammed in at the head.

"Sit with us today," she says. "The girls saved seats."

I'm not sure if they've saved a seat for me on purpose, or just for Harper. But Harper wants me to sit with her, and the other girls will include me if she does. Even if it's strange, for all of us. Even if Harper shifts back to aqua when she's with them.

"Come on," I say to Theo, reaching out my hand for him at the same time that I let myself be pulled by Harper. I want to sit with them, but I can't do it without him.

"There's no room," he says.

"We can bring over another chair."

"There aren't any."

"We'll squeeze. Share a seat with me." I look at him with pleading eyes.

"I'm fine sitting at *our* table." I don't get why he's not taking this chance to sit at the table we've both watched from a distance for years. He's being stubbornly, impossibly difficult old Theo.

"Enough indecision, kids. I'm starving." Harper pats her stomach and reaches dramatically toward the lunch line, which is extra-long. "Yum, waffles and sausage!"

I stand there like one of Dad's favorite Bernini sculptures—*Apollo and Daphne,* which he promised to take me to see one day in person in Rome—all twisted in different directions.

"C'mon," Harper says, dragging me along with her.

I could pull away. I could say no and go with Theo to our usual table.

Instead, I choose Harper.

I mouth "sorry" to Theo. But I can't look him in

the eyes. If I see the judgment there, I won't be able to enjoy my lunch.

Even so, I steal one last glance at him from where I sit with the Mermaids as I chew my waffle, not even tasting it.

And what I see on his face isn't judgment. It's hurt.

CHAPTER
five

I don't run into Theo the rest of the day.

The way I abandoned him at lunch pangs inside of me.

After school I look for him where we always meet up. Outside the main doors, to the left of the gate. He isn't there.

I wait until the frosty air bites through my gloves and boots, and my fingers and toes are numb. I wait until the stream of kids rushing past slows to a trickle, and then he comes.

"You waited." He seems surprised.

"Why wouldn't I?" Our moms started letting us walk to school together last year, in fifth grade. Now the rule is I'm allowed to walk anywhere on my own that's in reasonable distance from home. Like the Met, which is just across Central Park.

"After you ditched me at lunch, I wasn't so sure."

"C'mon, Theo. It's not like I didn't ask you to join. And people can have more than one friend, you know."

"But Chloe and Violet? Harper? Really?"

"They're fun."

"And I'm not?"

"That's not what I said, Theo."

"You kind of did, apparently. You told Harper you never do anything special for your birthday."

"Fine. Look, I'm sorry. That's not really what I meant." But I can't get the right tone of apology in my voice, and he's staring straight ahead, his nostrils flaring and his breath huffing out puffs of cold air.

We continue in silence, passing the Shooting Star diner, where some of the cooler kids from our grade go after school. I let my hair swing over my face, just in case Harper and the Mermaids are in there and might see me. As we weave down the busy sidewalks of Columbus Avenue, dodging kids on scooters and old people with walkers, Theo tells me about his idea for his NYC ART entry.

"You think I can make my self-portrait as a single panel from the *Adventures of Theo-Dare*?" he asks. "That would be something different, right? Make my entry stand out from the rest. Most kids are going to try to go all artsy and deep. And then you've got my superhero. *Wham-bam-kapow-pow!*"

"Probably," I agree. He launches into Theo-Dare's newest adventure, breaking into a fortified mansion to recover the largest ruby in the world, which was stolen from a museum by an expert jewelry thief for a billionaire gangster.

As I space out, I catch a glimpse of my reflection

in a store window. Do I really look like that? Flat and narrow, shoulders straining under the weight of my backpack, dark hair swinging into my face.

That's an interesting idea for a self-portrait—to sketch my reflection as I see it in a store window. I could snap a picture, but that would ruin it, take away how it makes me feel inside. Which is strange, and disconnected. Like my mind is not really in *that* body.

"Are you even listening, Georgia?" Theo asks. I look up, startled. He's a few steps ahead.

"Yeah, keep going."

The idea for a window reflection self-portrait fades as Theo plays out his story with voices and hand movements. I avoid turning my head so I don't catch my reflection again.

We turn off Columbus onto our street, West Eighty-Seventh, lined with brownstones and low-rise apartment buildings. You can tell which buildings have been bought and made fancier for single families and which are still divided into lots of apartments. The sidewalk is uneven in front of the buildings no one cares about. In some places, the squares of concrete have risen up to create little hills that Theo and I used to race over on our scooters.

Spindly tree branches stretch overhead. The roots break out of sad-looking patches of rocky soil, some still littered with fragments of discarded Christmas trees. Garbage pickup day means we have to weave single file around heaps of trash bags spilling their junk onto the street. Outside one of the crumbling brownstones, there's a large mattress, stained and wrapped in plastic. And an easy chair with itchy-looking green-and-gold fabric that's been scratched to pieces, maybe by a cat, leaking its insides.

We get to our building, and Theo's still talking: "So then, he finds this security badge, that's, like, the answer to all his problems. Or at least he thinks so. But when he goes to use it, he realizes it's super-encrypted, and he also needs fingerprint verification. When he doesn't give that, it sets off an alarm—"

I interrupt Theo to wave and call hello to Mrs. Velandry. She's the old lady who lives in the first floor apartment of our building, a low-rise tucked behind the fancy buildings on Central Park West with their doormen and elevator attendants.

We don't have door people, but Mrs. Velandry is kind of like a door person, the way she sits there all day, watching people coming and going. Her living room is next to the entrance. Mom says she has mild agoraphobia—a fear of going outside. So she's there. Almost all the time.

She's also our landlady. Her husband's family owned the building; he grew up and died here, and left it to her. When I was younger and Mom was working late, Mrs. Velandry would keep an eye on me. But I had to go to her apartment—she wouldn't come to ours.

Even though Mom lets me stay home by myself now, I still like going to Mrs. Velandry's apartment.

She's a good cook, and she'll always offer me a bowl of soup or spaghetti for dinner. Plus her dogs, Olive and especially Royal, are practically my own.

Dad adopted Royal, a golden Shih Tzu (named for his favorite color, royal blue) as a puppy, when he first moved into the building. But then he met Mom, who is allergic to dogs, and Mrs. Velandry offered to keep Royal for Dad when they got married. A couple of years later, Mrs. Velandry bought Olive at a pet shop, because she saw her in the window and felt sorry for her, and she thought Royal was lonely, too. Olive is a brown-and-white Shih Tzu and she barks all the time. Unlike Royal, who indulges his younger sister and tries to ignore her noise like we all do.

Royal is seventeen now, and mostly blind and maybe deaf. He doesn't like to walk, even though Mrs. Velandry has a dog walker take them out four times a day, so the building's vestibule always smells like pee, because that's where he loses control of his bladder. No cleaning products can mask the icky smell. But it's worth it, because Dad loved Royal, and so do I.

Mrs. Velandry waves at us with two hands: one for me, one for Theo.

I use a key I wear on a leather cord around my neck to unlock the outer door.

I pinch my nose closed against the pee smell as Theo and I dart through the inner door and into the lobby, across the chipped and dull marble floor. We cover our ears to the racket of Olive barking. The blast of the radiator brings warmth back to my fingers and cheeks.

"G, I'm still telling you the Theo-Dare story," Theo shouts above Olive's racket.

"Yeah, let me just say hi to the dogs, and then she'll stop."

Theo glumly takes a seat at the base of the stairs. I ring Mrs. Velandry's door and wait for her to turn all three locks.

The dogs rush to me, jumping up on my legs, licking my hands. Olive quits her barking to sniff me wildly, wagging her tail. Royal plops himself on my feet. I scoop him up for a cuddle, give him a kiss on top of his head, and hand him back to Mrs. Velandry.

"Good day?" she asks.

"Not bad," I say.

"Come by for some zucchini bread later—you, too, Theo," she says as I head to the stairs.

"Thanks," we call.

"More Theo-Dare?" he asks, standing up.

"Yeah," I say, taking the steps two at a time. Our building has a rickety elevator that's painfully slow and gets stuck at the worst times. I don't have the patience.

I'm a few inches taller than Theo, and faster. I could race up these stairs to my apartment on the top floor and leave him a flight behind if I wanted. But I stay only a few steps ahead. Trying to focus on his story.

We get to Theo's floor. Five. I keep walking.

"See ya later!" I don't look back.

"But, G, don't you want to hear the rest? Sketch through some NYC ART ideas together?" I hear worry in Theo's voice.

He's worried because I'm breaking our routine. Every day after school we go to his apartment, have a snack, do our homework. Draw. Paint. Play with Krypto.

But today. Today is different.

I want to be home.

Without Theo.

"Too much work. Gotta focus." I take off up the last flight of stairs. Lightning speed. Super G speed.

No time to feel regret over the confusion and disappointment left in my wake.

CHAPTER

six

The landing outside our apartment door looks like a warehouse.

Mounds of flattened cardboard packing boxes, empty painting crates, and Styrofoam peanuts cover the floor.

It did not look like this when I left for school this morning.

Our sixth-floor apartment is called PH, or penthouse, which sounds fancy but just means it's the top floor of the building. The reason it worked as an artist's studio for Dad is that it was built on the roof, with a double-height living room that has windows facing south. Plus the balcony was a total bonus.

It felt magical, growing up in Dad's art studio. The *New York Times* once did a profile of Dad's Sunday routine. They wrote something like: "There's no clear line between Hank Rosenbloom's home and studio, especially on Sunday mornings when the aroma of coffee brewing and French toast on the griddle fills the space, momentarily masking the smell of paints and oils, enticing his six-year-old daughter to take a seat at his drafting table to enjoy her brunch, all crafted by the hand of the artist."

The sentence is long so the words get jumbled in my mind. But it captures the feeling of how our Sunday mornings *were*: that mixture of art and French toast.

The framed article hangs on our kitchen wall above the whiteboard where Mom and I scribble notes to each other. Like our life with Dad can be framed and admired—remembered as part of the past. Mom's French toast is such a poor comparison to Dad's that she doesn't even try. It's more likely to be instant oatmeal and egg whites. Even the door to our balcony has been locked since then. I have no idea where Mom keeps the key. That magical feeling of living in Dad's studio has turned ordinary.

Bubble Wrap pops under my feet as I step over boxes to get to the front door. I use the other key on my leather cord for this door, but it's already unlocked, which means Mom is home.

There's an even bigger surprise inside: Dad's paintings. After almost two years of living with bare walls, the shock of seeing Dad's splashes of color everywhere makes my head spin. I half expect to see him standing at his easel, humming along to opera, gliding his paintbrush across a canvas.

There's *G in Blue*, a portrait of me. A smallish square panel that shows me as an ultramarine blue triangle, floating against a white background.

Dad said ultramarine is the most expensive blue pigment, which is why he chose it to paint me. During the Renaissance it was made from the semiprecious stone lapis lazuli and was worth more than gold. Old master artists used it for painting the dress of Mary. It was one of Dad's favorite colors: a deep, brilliant blue. Like royal blue. But I don't know if that blue is the color I'd choose for myself. I don't know what color I'd choose.

All I see for me now is a deep moody gray. Charcoal.

There's *Glimpse of Light*, with its stripes and layers of yellows: canary, daffodil, lemon.

Figure in the Dusk, which shows Mom as a burgundy cylinder against a black background. I wonder why he chose that color for Mom. Burgundy, made up of pigments like red ochre, brambleberry, oxblood.

I try to see it in her as she calls from where she's seated at the table, "Hi, honey!"

The reality of what she's doing—hard at work on an exhibition about Dad—fades his presence from the room.

She doesn't even ask me how my day was or look up from the notes she's making on a legal pad. Her hair is pulled back into a messy bun and she's wearing her thick tortoiseshell glasses, which means she hasn't showered and she's tired and she might not shower or put in her contact lenses for days.

I don't see her as burgundy, but as dull beige. Fawn or taupe on a good day.

Maybe the burgundy drained out of her when Dad died.

"What are all those boxes? It looks like a tornado blew through here."

"Major crunch time for the exhibition. I just got them from storage, and I'm working through it here, and then bringing what I need over to the Met." Mom looks up, but not at me. At the piles on the tables. "All these early sketches and notebooks that we'd almost forgotten about. Some are from when he was around your age."

"Can I see?" I walk over to the table and set down my backpack.

"It's a total mess." Mom rubs at her eyes and pulls her bun tighter. "This early stuff was just thrown into boxes with no rhyme or reason. Most of it, I've never seen before, and the ones I've gotten through today aren't even dated. Take a look—but not at this pile, which I've already gone through. Tell me if you find anything interesting."

All of Dad's art is interesting to me. Because for ten years, *I* was in his life. I was there when he made his art. I saw him draw and paint and step back and make changes and throw things out and start over and, finally, decide a piece was done.

I start sifting through the stacks of papers in front of me. Mom sits back in her chair and looks out the window, like her attention is caught by something out there. "Remember how Dad used to make those mixed-up animal drawings with you?"

Of course I do. He'd start a sketch by making a head, and then fold the paper, and then I'd draw the body, and fold and give it back to him to do the legs and feet. And then I'd unfold the whole thing and we'd end up with a crazy image. I keep a folder of those mixed-up animal drawings in my desk drawer. Sometimes we'd play it with Theo, too. But recently when Theo started one and passed it over to me, I said no. The game isn't as fun as it used to be.

"I found one today," she says, handing it to me. "That's what made me think of it. Not sure how it got boxed in with all these papers."

I look at the drawing, on a piece of yellow construction paper that's old enough to have faded along the edges. I smile: Dad had drawn a penguin head, I drew a butterfly body, and he'd finished it with elephant feet.

"Maybe that's what I could do." Draw myself as a mixed-up animal for NYC ART. A girl with a unicorn horn, a blue jay's head, dragon wings, a lion's mane, and a mermaid's tail.

"Do for what?" Mom asks.

I tell her that the NYC ART theme was announced today.

"Self-portrait!" She leans toward me. Focusing

on *me* for the first time since I got home. "How lucky! That's the best theme, isn't it? Last year, what was it? Growth or metamorphosis or something? Too obscure. So, what are you going to do?"

"I don't know."

"Well, I can't wait to see what you come up with." She opens her mouth to say something else, then stops and says softly, "Wouldn't it be special to have your first art show at the Met at the same time as Dad's?"

Sure, that'd be great, but what if I don't come up with anything?

What if I *can't* come up with anything?

"I just think—I'm not going to enter."

As soon as the words are out there, I know I mean it. Entering is a choice I can make. I might have to make a self-portrait for class, but NYC ART is optional. An option I'm not going to take.

"Really?" She studies my face like she's trying to figure out what I'm thinking. "But you've been looking forward to it for years."

Dad always took me and Theo to see the NYC ART exhibit in the spring at the Met. We'd walk across the park; he'd point out the daffodils and forsythia and cherry blossom trees. Sometimes it would be one of the first real bright, sunny days of spring, the kind of day that makes you want to stay outside forever. Other times it would still be chilly and wet, and the museum, with its perfectly regulated temperatures, would feel cozy.

Either way, we loved seeing those kids' artworks on the walls of the education center at the Met— their names and titles and ages and schools printed on labels next to their pieces—and imagining the day it'd be our turn.

I look back down at the mixed-up animal, a spot of bright yellow next to those piles of papers, the lines blurring before my eyes. "I don't know. . . . I don't want to talk about it. I'm just hungry."

She springs to action, to do something that can make me feel better. Right away. "Snack? Sliced apple and cheddar?"

"Sure." I push aside a stack of papers to make more room at the table.

"Careful, sweetie!" Mom's voice turns shrill. She's worried I might damage something.

"I just need a place to eat!" My words come out angrier and sharper than I mean them. Sometimes—a *lot* of times—it's like these random pieces of paper with Dad's pencil marks and brushstrokes are more important to her than me, her living, breathing daughter.

Mom winces like I've hurt her. She turns to the kitchen. I almost wish she'd yell back. To tell me she's as sad and confused as I am. But, no—she's got her work, her job keeping Dad's memory alive.

While she's in the kitchen, I flip through the papers in one of the piles. Some sheets have just a few lines on them, random shapes or scribbles that look like Dad trying to work out ideas.

But then, toward the bottom of the pile, there's something hard.

A portfolio.

Not just any portfolio, but the kind Dad always used, with a black cover and clear plastic sleeves inside for drawings.

I thought all his sketchbooks and portfolios were in one box together. Apparently, not this one.

I pull it out from the bottom of the pile, flip open the cover, and take a deep breath.

This is definitely Dad's. His name is on the inside front cover in silver Sharpie, where he wrote his name on all his portfolios.

Maybe this is one that nobody knows about.

And maybe I'm the only person ever to see it.

Besides Dad.

CHAPTER

seven

The first drawing is of a baby, sleeping peacefully in someone's arms.

Not just any baby.

Me. I see it written clear as day, in Dad's cursive on the lower back corner of the page, when I turn over the plastic sleeve: *G, 7 months.*

Without looking at each page, I can tell from the thickness that the portfolio is nearly full—with drawings of me.

I flip through. There's me at thirteen months, eighteen months, twenty-nine months. The initial G and the age written on the lower back corner of each one.

My first instinct is to call out to Mom. She's still in the kitchen, her phone pinging away in a texting exchange.

Good. More time for me to be alone with the portfolio.

Because I don't actually want to call for her. I don't want to share this or ask her about it. I want to look at in my room, by myself.

If I tell her, she'll make it official. Catalogue it, enter it into a database, conserve it, write an article about it. Take it away like she took away Dad's paintings.

But this is *me*. It *should* be my own private thing to look at. For just a little while, at least.

I slip the portfolio into my backpack, sling it over my shoulder, and head to the kitchen.

"I'll take my snack in my room."

"You sure?" Mom asks as she hands the plate to me. She's probably happy to have me out of her way so she can focus on her work.

I close my door and clear my desk, pushing aside sketchbooks and mason jars crammed with pencils and markers. I switch on the desk lamp, lighting up the bulletin board over my desk. It's filled with drawings and sketches I've made over the years, and Polaroids I took of Mom and Dad with a camera they once gave me for Hanukkah— the two of them smiling at me from our living room couch, a side view of them arm in arm on the beach, the backs of their heads looking at Dad's art, Dad's ice skates—and a funny series of Theo cuddling Krypto. The blue faux fur van Gogh hat from my cringey Halloween costume peers at me over the edge of a bookshelf, stuffed in between my books and LEGO sets I used to build.

I pull out the portfolio, placing it on my desk next to the snack. My heart flutters as I turn the pages. They're like kisses from Dad, blown across time. Dad had watched me, *seen* me, loved me enough to study me, to draw me, to capture me in pencil on paper. And I had no idea.

The drawings are different than *G in Blue,* the triangle portrait of me in our living room. Sure, that painting is pretty, but the triangle could be anything. Not like these drawings, which are figurative representations of me. Which couldn't be anything *but* me.

The portfolio has twenty sleeves, and all but the last three are full. I'm sad for the empty sleeves—the ones he didn't get a chance to fill.

Some images are drawn super loose, just a few lines. Toddler me, running, jumping, swinging, like Dad was figuring out how to capture me in motion.

Some are detailed face drawings. In *G, age 7,* I'm looking straight on, into the eyes of the person—Dad—drawing me. I like how strong and confident I look there.

The last page jolts me. Because, at first glance, the drawing looks like it could be of me now. The style is in between detailed, figurative, and looser, more abstract.

It's simple, using a few spare lines to capture

the image of this girl in three-quarter profile. She's sitting in a chair, like the cozy womb chair in the corner of our living room by the bookshelves. Head bent, hair falling across her cheek, like she's reading a book in her lap. Her eyebrows knit together, lips pursed in concentration.

I like the energy of the girl in that drawing. You can tell she's absorbed in her book. Not aware that someone—Dad—is watching, drawing her—me.

This is me. This is who I am.

My truth.

A shiver runs down my spine, like the ghost of Dad returned and did this sketch only yesterday.

The writing on the lower back corner of the page confirms: *G, age 10*.

Two years ago.

This must be the last drawing Dad ever made of me. Right after I turned ten.

A great, awful ache fills my chest.

If only I could reach back through the pages of this portfolio to that ten-year-old version of me, to tell her to hold on to her father a little longer. To enjoy every moment they have together because it won't last forever.

But then I notice something else on the back of this page.

A series of dots. Pencil points.

Like the points of stars that make an asterism.

The pencil points are faint, not super definite. Like they could just be the pencil marks showing through from the front of the paper. You could almost miss them if you didn't know what they might be.

But with that split second of recognition, of *knowing*, my teeth chatter like with fever chills, and I'm suddenly so cold that I wrap my soft gray wool baby blanket from my bed over my shoulders.

I slide the drawing out of the sleeve and run my fingers over the lines of the paper, ever so gently, careful not to rub away the pencil marks. I lift it up to the light of my desk lamp. To see if the pencil points are random. Or if they mean something.

And against the light, it's pretty clear to me.

Those pencil points match up with the lines of the drawing of me on the other side of the page: one point for the top of my head, one for the tip of my nose, one for the back of my head, two points along my body, two more for my feet, and three points to show the book I'm holding.

Ten pencil points in total. Ten, maybe, for the age I was when Dad drew this.

The last asterism.

This paper, this drawing, *G, age 10,* here in my hands, might be proof.

Proof that it was me. *I'm* the last asterism.

Or at least, I think this drawing proves that.

Mom's voice on a phone call echoes from the living room.

My brain tells me I should show her the drawing. So we can announce to the world that we know what Hank Rosenbloom's fourth asterism was meant to be. Hang it in the Met exhibition along with the finished paintings.

But there's so much of Dad that I share with the world. This is one piece of him that's private, that's mine. It's like Dad left this portfolio, this drawing, behind on purpose for me to discover, and I don't have to share it with anybody. Not even Mom. Or Theo.

Unless I choose to. When I'm ready.

If I'm ready.

I slip *G, age 10* into my desk drawer along with the mixed-up animals. And the tiny corner of the photograph with Dad's toe in it.

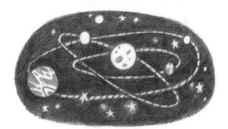

CHAPTER
eight

Mom knocks on my door later that night, while I'm reading. Usually she just peeks in to say good night. But tonight she takes a seat on the edge of my bed. On the lacy-trimmed cover that I've had since forever, which I refuse to change for a new one even though it's worn through and torn in places. I like how soft and familiar it is. That can't be replaced.

"Hey." I set down my book, realizing I'm getting tired.

"How are you?" She puts a hand on my arm—

something she never seems to do anymore. It's kind of comforting. But still, I shrug and pull away. Dad used to sing me songs every night, and then Mom would come in and rub my back and sit with me while I got close to falling asleep. I didn't like her to sing to me because her voice wasn't as good as Dad's.

Mom crosses her arms and I wish I could lean into her and wrap my arms around her neck, that she'd pull me close into a tight, warm hug. It's just, that's not what we do anymore.

"I suppose I've been too distracted by my work lately," she begins.

I sit up higher in my bed. "You could say that."

"I know, and I'm sorry. But I'm also sad to hear you say that you're not going to enter NYC ART. Are you sure?"

"I don't know. I just feel like nothing's working."

"Oh, honey." Mom wraps me into that tight hug I thought I wanted, but it doesn't feel right. Not like it used to. I don't hug back. "Have you tried?"

I shake my head. "And Theo . . . he's just so competitive with me."

"About what?" Mom squints at me, like she's trying to see into my head.

"About everything." I turn away from her, wanting to hide my face. I don't know how to begin to explain how complicated my feelings are about Theo. That I love him and am jealous of him all at the same time. I know she'll just say it's normal to feel that way with a best friend, that I should value his friendship. "Even with friends. I'm making some new ones."

"Oh. Like who?"

"The new girl, Harper Willis. Her parents own one of Dad's paintings!"

"That name does sound familiar . . . Willis. Oh, yes, Dominic and Olivia Willis. Big contemporary art collectors. They have two of Dad's paintings, actually."

"Which ones?" Harper only mentioned one.

"They have one of the Bird series—*Charcoal*

on Green. And the first asterism, *Bird in the Tree*. They're lending both to the exhibit, so they'll be coming over to the Met soon."

My heart skips a few beats at that. I hope I'll get to see the paintings in person. "She actually invited me to hang out on Friday."

"Lucky you—the paintings should still be there. I've met the parents briefly; they know their art. Is she nice?"

Nice is not the word that I'd use to describe Harper. "Well, she's super cool and confident. And totally down-to-earth. She asked me to draw designs for this Valentine's Day charity card sale she's doing, which is why I'm going over there—to plan."

"Wouldn't Theo be a good help on drawing card designs?"

Ugh. It's not like we're still five and she can just suggest that I invite another friend along to a play date. "Actually, Chloe Chen and Violet Avilez are helping, too. Not with drawing, but the whole sale thing. They're Harper's best friends."

Mom knows what I mean by Chloe and Violet without me having to explain.

"Let me guess. Theo doesn't fit in with those girls?"

I nod.

"Do you?"

I shrug. I don't know yet.

"Having other friends is nice. And important. But Theo—he's a dear, old friend. And Harriet, too. I can't imagine what I'd do without her. Without them. Everything's been so hard. We need all the support we can get."

And without her saying it, I know what she means. She means that Theo will support and be there for me no matter what. The Mermaids— who knows. But what about feeling stuck with the old and dependable? What about wanting to try something different, new?

"The next few months are going to be extra-challenging," she continues. "I need to focus on

Dad's show. The reviews we get will determine his legacy. It's not just a matter of critical success, honey. It's also a financial issue. If we get good reviews, it brings up the value of Dad's art. Everything . . . I'm lucky to have this opportunity from the Met, and I need *you* to understand."

I roll my eyes and grimace. This is what I hate about the art world. It's like these people don't even care about Dad. The value of his art is all that matters. The price.

Mom sees the look on my face. "Oh, honey, I shouldn't put this on you. But there are some realities you need to understand. Doing this all alone—it's a lot."

I clench my teeth. I want to tell her she's not all alone. She has me. I wish there was something I could do to help. But I'm afraid I'm part of her problem—raising me, alone.

"But I came in here to talk about you. Not me. *You.* And NYC ART. Dad would've been so proud of you for entering."

"Maybe," I whisper. No one really knows how Dad would've felt.

"Does this have anything to do with what I asked Theo the other night—about the Q&A for the catalogue?"

I look away from her and pick up my book again, but can't focus on the words.

"Because I meant it when I said I'd like you to participate, too. It didn't come out the right way when I asked. It was like one of those conversations I had in my head with you, and I forgot that we hadn't actually had it yet, so then when I asked him, and realized I hadn't asked you . . ." She scratches her forehead like she's trying to clear up the muddle in her brain. But I don't say anything to make this easier for her.

"Oh, honey, I'm getting this all wrong. I'll be proud of you no matter what, or who, you choose to become. Dad would be, too. Entering NYC ART— it'd be nice, but it doesn't define who you are."

Her words wash over me. I'm not even thinking

about NYC ART anymore. Instead, I'm thinking about the drawing I found. *G, age 10.*

I could tell her about it right now. Show her what I'm pretty sure is the asterism sketch on the back. I could get all the credit for proving what Dad planned to do.

Only if I showed her right now—I wouldn't get credit at all. I'd just be handing her something I found on the table. A few pencil points on the back of the paper don't prove anything on their own. It was just a feeling I got.

Mom always says instinct is the initial spark for art historians to make their discoveries, but then they need to do research to prove that instinct is correct.

Someone has to do the research to prove what those pencil points mean.

And that someone, why can't it be me?

Later, after I hear her door close, I tiptoe out of my room. I clutch Dad's portfolio—minus *G, age 10*—to my chest.

I slide it back into the pile where I found it. One of the piles Mom said she hadn't looked through yet. The portfolio has been in storage all these years with stuff she said she's never even seen. For all I know, she's never seen this portfolio before, either. So she won't know that one drawing is missing.

nine

At first, every time I look at G, *age 10* in my desk drawer, I feel a spark of connection to Dad. Like we have a secret between us.

But as the days pass, the good feeling about taking the drawing fades. Instead, it makes me feel alone—more alone than ever. The one person alive who knows this secret thing.

It's like if a tree falls in a forest and no one's there to hear it, does it make a sound? If no one knows about Dad's last asterism sketch, does it mean anything?

Part of me longs to tell Theo, who's an expert at

figuring out these kinds of situations. Theo-Dare would know how to prove the sketch is what I think it is.

But real Theo would be a do-gooder, responsible—try to convince me that the drawing is too important to keep to myself. He'd want me to tell Mom. And then it would no longer be *my* discovery. Or he'd try to help me, and it would become *our* discovery, not mine alone.

So I decide not to tell anyone until I have proof.

Every time I'm home alone the rest of the week, I look through the folders and papers and books on our big table.

Mom continues to separate the materials into two piles: 1) bring to the Met for the exhibit, and 2) put back in the archives. So I have to be careful not to mess up anything.

And nothing I find seems important, anyway. Like Mom said, most of it is early work. But I keep looking. For what, I don't know. I hope I'll know it when I see it.

I search the Internet for articles about Dad's asterisms and look at the Met's and Whitney's descriptions of the asterism paintings on their websites, but none of them mention anything about sketches for the paintings on the back of drawings.

Even if I do find proof, then what? It'd probably be too late to make it into the exhibit. But that's not why I care, anyway. Proving the drawing is a sketch for the last asterism is something I want to do for me—not for the world.

By Thursday afternoon, Mom's teaching day at Columbia, I've found nothing.

I'm alone at home after school, except for Dad's paintings. I look at all of them propped up around the room, wondering if one of them can tell me something. If they hold any clues.

What if he made asterism points on the back of the canvases? I've heard of artists sometimes doing that—sketching directly on the back of a canvas. Maybe he made points on the back of the unfinished canvas that mirror the ones on the back of G, *age 10*. That would prove that the drawing is a sketch.

I know I've seen the back of that canvas, during the time that Mom had flipped it around so we didn't have to look at its blankness. But I wasn't looking for evidence then. I didn't look closely to see if Dad drew anything on the back. And if Mom noticed anything, she didn't say.

I go up to the canvas, which is taller than me. Six feet—about the same height as Dad. It's been collecting dust in the corner for almost two years. There's literally a line of it along the edges.

I put my fingertips to the frame to tilt the canvas forward, and a poof of dust tickles my nose, making me sneeze. I'm mindful to sneeze away from the canvas and into my elbow. Even though it's just an empty blank, it's still Dad's work, and I don't want my sneeze particles to contaminate it.

It's heavier than I expected. It almost slips forward on top of me. I use both hands to brace it and peek around to the back.

There's nothing. Just clean, untouched canvas. The raw edges stapled to the wood frame. I lean it back against the wall. But just because he didn't sketch on the back of this canvas doesn't mean he didn't on the others.

Next I check *G in Blue*. The portrait of me as a triangle is much smaller. Gingerly, I touch the edge of the frame, careful not to get any fingerprints on the paint. I've been trained since I was a baby to look, not touch. Sometimes Dad would let me touch paintings. Back then it was okay if I accidentally smudged something because he was there to fix it. Now I wouldn't risk it. Of course, it's been so many years since Dad painted it, there's little chance it's still wet, even though oils take forever to dry.

I tip the painting forward and peek at the back. Again, no marks. Nothing.

I check the other paintings—*Figure in the Dusk, Glimpse of Light, Self-Portrait in Brown,* and *The Dimness of Being*.

Nothing. Nothing, and more nothing.

Which makes total sense: Dad wouldn't make points on the backs of these canvases; they're not asterism paintings.

He made the points on the back of the drawing of me. Maybe what I need to find are *drawings* for the other asterism paintings—not finished canvases, not sketches or scraps of paper. Drawings, like *G, age 10*. There should be one of Mom, one of Dad, and one of a bird.

And I know just where to start looking. Mom has her own special drawing from Dad, like Theo has his. A drawing Dad made of her when they first met.

The drawing is under glass in a delicate gold picture frame, propped up on our fireplace mantel. In between the cross-stitch sampler Mom's mom made for my parents when they got married, with their names entwined in a tree, and a black-and-white photograph of Mom and Dad with me as a baby, taken by one of Dad's photographer friends.

I walk over to the fireplace. The thin gold frame

is light and cool in my hands. I'm about to take it over to the table, where I can set it down and slide open the frame, when I hear footsteps outside our apartment and the front door handle turns. Mom's home early. *Shoot.* "Hello!" she calls out as I race to put the picture back on the mantel.

I'm standing there totally awkward by the fireplace. Mom gives me a puzzled look. "Everything okay? What're you up to?"

"Um, I'm just—I was—" Staring at me from the corner of the living room, next to the balcony door, is the large case for Dad's telescope. I point to it. "I was thinking it'd be fun to try using Dad's telescope again one night. You know. We haven't used it since—"

Mom's hand is to her mouth and she looks like she's seen a ghost. "Oh, honey." She drops her leather workbag and strides over to me without even taking off her boots or coat. She pulls me into a hug.

The kind of hug that could be comforting if it's what I wanted right now. But what I really want is more time alone to look at the back of her drawing and continue my search.

"Mom, where's the key to the balcony door, anyway?" I ask, pulling away.

"Oh, gosh. It must be here somewhere. Maybe in my jewelry box, or my office desk. I don't know. Everything's foggy from those days. I promise, I'll find it by the time the weather turns nice. And the windows need to be cleaned, don't they?"

It's not like I think I'll find anything helpful to my search out on the balcony. Looking at the actual stars isn't what matters. Dad made up his own asterisms, after all.

But, maybe, if I look at the stars through his telescope, it'll tell me something about what he was thinking, how he was thinking. Maybe, using Dad's telescope again will feel like being with him. Because just like the unfinished canvas for the last asterism started to fade into the wall, so have my memories of him. The things that don't always show in his art. The things that made him my dad.

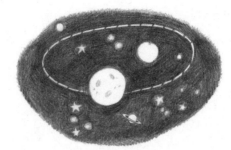

CHAPTER

ten

In science we're doing a unit on astronomy. Dr. Anders tells us that the sun is ninety-three million miles away, and that the light from the sun takes about eight minutes to reach the Earth. So the sunlight we see happened eight minutes earlier.

Eight minutes doesn't seem like a lot of time, but things that can change the course of your entire life can happen in those four hundred and eighty seconds.

With an eight-minute delay, I could change my

decision to take Dad's drawing and hide it in my desk drawer. Because Friday morning, the portfolio with the drawings of me is no longer on the table, which means Mom's put it somewhere else, and I've missed my chance to put G, *age 10* back where it belongs—if I wanted to.

If I had an eight-minute delay, I could've chosen not to sit with Harper at lunch on Monday. Because the next day, she waved me over to their table. Even though I could see across the room that Theo was saving me a seat at our old table, I didn't want to say no to Harper. And that's how I begin sitting with the Mermaids.

Every time I chose Harper over Theo that week, it pushed him farther away. I didn't even see him after school because he was busy doing set design for the middle school musical. Walking home without Theo, I felt like I'd forgotten something. I kept stopping to check my backpack and make sure my homework planner and books were inside.

And I haven't made the choice yet to tell Mr.

Butterweit and Theo that I've decided not to enter NYC ART. Telling them will make my decision official. But I know I have to do it soon to give Mr. B the chance to enter someone else's work.

Art looms on my schedule for Friday afternoon, my second-to-last period of the day, before science.

During free-draw period at the start of class, Mr. B sets out the hand mirrors again. "Self-portrait" is written in large bubble letters across the whiteboard. A reminder that even if I don't want to submit an entry for the competition, I have to make *something*—for class, for my grade.

All I can think of is a mixed-up animal. I pull out a tray of Cray-pas oil pastels, which are like softer versions of crayons. They're smooth on the paper, and their effect is like paint.

First my favorite blue-green color to make a mermaid tail, highlighted with curlicues in glittery silver. In my art I can become one of the Mermaids. I get that flow in my hand—the flow that's missing when I try to draw my actual self.

I'm working on the outlines of the unicorn horn and bird head when Harper plunks down into her seat next to me.

"Ugh, I'm so late." She pulls out her sketchbook. "Dr. Markham made me have this psychobabble meeting about how I'm adjusting to my new life. I'm all *what*? I'm not *new* here anymore. Seriously. You New York people just like to talk and talk."

I laugh. I had my own Dr. Markham "psychobabble" meetings in fourth grade. About Dad. Dr. Markham still asks to have check-ins with me. And she gives me sympathetic looks whenever she sees me, like we have a special connection.

"What're you working on?" Harper twists her hair into a long rope, then coils it into a messy bun with a pencil through it. Maybe that's why I like her—I don't even need to talk; she can carry on a conversation by herself. "Oh, that's so cute! A mermaid. With, what's that—a unicorn horn? Super cool, Georgia! Can we use that for one of the Valentine's cards? Bring that idea to our meeting!"

Right. Our planning meeting at her house after school today. I nod and swallow, wanting to tell her that a mixed-up animal isn't something I can share with the whole school.

Mr. B dims the light to signal the start of class. "Today we're going to continue to look at self-portraits, to figure out how to draw what you actually see. To notice specific details of facial features, such as shapes, lines, and spatial relationships. How do artists use their technical awareness to render themselves with authenticity?"

A self-portrait by the seventeenth-century Dutch artist Rembrandt lights up the screen. The version at the Met, which reminds me of Dad, since we used to go see the painting together.

"Rembrandt painted about forty self-portraits during his lifetime. He painted this one nine years before he died. He was fifty-four years old—what was considered an old man in those days."

My breath catches. Dad was fifty-four when he died, and everyone said how young he was.

"Rembrandt suffered great sadness," Mr. B continues. "He'd lost his wife, a child, his students. He was bankrupt. Yet he examines himself in the mirror and paints as he sees himself, with truth and sincerity. He doesn't try to make himself look better than he was. That's the Truth—the authenticity—I want you all to find. Seeing yourselves for who you really are and presenting that true self to the world."

What comes into my head is not who I really am, but the worst possible way to think of Dad: sick, a collapsed version of himself, in the hospital bed, tubes going in and out of his body. His hair had fallen out, brown and red spots speckled his skull. His skin was paper-thin, the veins like road maps in his hands.

His hands, which had been strong enough to lift the wood frame of a stretcher and pull canvas tight across, stapling it to the wood. Hands that could make magic with pencil on paper, paintbrush on canvas. In the end those hands were so weak, they could barely hold mine. But he reached for me with those hands, wanting to pull me close. To hug me.

The most awful part was that I was afraid to touch him. Afraid the cancer and drugs and radiation in his body were contagious, or that I'd knock an IV line out of his hand. Afraid of how different hugging him would be.

If only I could go back—not just eight minutes, but months, years. If only I could've not been afraid.

"Next time you're at the Met, remember to visit this Rembrandt," Mr. B says. "In person you can really notice how extraordinary the eyes are. The eye on the right is hazy, distorted, and the one on the left is in focus, looking at us directly. Why would Rembrandt have done that?"

Mr. B waits. He's not going to help us out here.

As usual, Theo has an answer. "It shows us what he was feeling inside. He was old and having a hard time. But he was also strong and confident. Bold."

"Yes. For your own self-portraits, think about

your eyes, what they can tell us about your feelings. It might not just be one thing—but two or more feelings. Maybe even conflicting feelings, like Rembrandt: full of loss, and yet still strong."

"What are my eyes saying?" Harper whispers to me, pulling me away from Mr. B's ideas as she wiggles and crosses her eyes.

I hold in a giggle, watching her cross and uncross her eyes. But then she stops, suddenly, and her eyes go really wide at something on the screen. And I know before I even turn to look, that it's something about me. Because Luca Banks points and says "Georgia!"

It's not actually me—it's him—the van Gogh self-portrait with a bandaged ear, blue fur trapper hat and all. The one I dressed up as for Halloween. I feel my cheeks burn hot and slap my hand over my eyes so I don't have to see all the stares on me.

But I hear my name *Georgia Georgia Georgia* in whispers and snorts of laughter around me until Mr. B, confused by the reaction, calls for quiet.

I don't even hear what he has to say about van Gogh—something about choice of color, prominent brushstrokes, a feeling of disconnection. All I hear is the words Harper whispers in my ear, "You were such a nerd!" I shake my head in protest, but inside, I silently agree.

After what feels like hours, Mr. B finally turns to another image. Frida Kahlo, the great Mexican artist. Her thick, dark hair is piled on top of her head, her bushy eyebrows meet in the middle of her forehead, and she has the trace of a mustache.

"Frida Kahlo made one hundred forty-three paintings in her life, and fifty-five of those are self-portraits. Do the math: that's a large percentage of her work." Mr. B scrolls through a few slides. One shows two images of her in the same painting. In another, she's framed by a decorative pattern, including birds. Dad would've liked that one.

"There's a famous quote by Kahlo about why she paints herself: 'I paint self-portraits because I am so often alone, because I am the person I know best.'"

That confuses me, because I also feel like I'm often alone, but I don't think I'm the person I know best. I don't think I know myself at all.

At the end of art class, I turn back to my half-drawn mixed-up animal.

Maybe each part of that animal shows a different part of me: the unicorn horn is the artist-me; the blue-jay head is the daughter-of-Hank-me; the mermaid tail is the friend-of-Harper-me . . . and on and on.

There are so many different versions of me:

The "me" who is my mother's daughter, who was my father's daughter.

The "me" who wants to follow in my father's footsteps, but isn't sure she can.

The "me" who's always been best friends with Theo but is pushing him away.

And the new "me," who's becoming friends with Harper.

But which one is my truth—the real me?

The problem with the mixed-up animal is that

it has nothing at the center. There's no truth at its core—it's just a jumble of different parts.

Still, it could be the self-portrait that I hand in to Mr. B for my classwork.

The one thing I do know is that it's time for me to tell him I'm not entering NYC ART. I take a deep breath and wait near Mr. B's desk until the room empties.

"Hey." I twist the straps of my backpack into a spiral.

"How're you doing, Georgia?" He looks up from the notes he's making in his attendance book. "I heard some whispers of your name in class. Anything you want to talk about?"

"Not about that," I say, looking down, feeling the burn come back to my cheeks.

"Okay," he says, but he doesn't sound convinced. "You know I'm here if you ever want to talk. How's your self-portrait coming along?"

"Actually," I look up. The simple words rush off my tongue, "I don't want to enter NYC ART."

"You don't want to enter?" he repeats, like he's trying to process the impossible.

Disappointment weighs heavy in my stomach, like I've just eaten a slice of pizza too many. It would be so easy to take it back. To say that's not what I meant. But I do mean it. I don't want to enter this competition. Not with a self-portrait.

I shake my head. He's quiet, waiting for more of an explanation, but I can't give one. So I bite the inside of my cheek and squeeze my hands together.

"You still have time, if you change your mind. Take this weekend to think it over, and let's check in next week. We can make a time to sit down and go over your ideas together."

I just shake my head again and turn to run out of the room. I don't want his kindness. Not right now.

Theo's leaning against the wall outside the art studio, waiting for me to walk to science.

"Long time, no see." He brushes his fingers

through his hair, which stands up higher than usual. And his glasses are clean—I can actually see his eyes. He smells different, too. Not like hummus and pretzels, but a soapy scent, like hair gel. "Krypto and I miss you. Lunch isn't the same without you."

I shrug. "Neither is walking home alone. I guess you've been busy."

"Yeah, can't wait until these sets are finished. Then I get home late and draw Theo-Dare panels. Still haven't figured out which one I'm going to use for the final entry."

"I'm sure they're all great."

"Want to come by later and see them? Help me choose?"

"Not today. I'm busy."

"Doing what?"

"You know, the Valentine's Day cards with Harper."

"Oh, that." Theo rolls his eyes—as if set design isn't a waste of precious art-making time, but card design is. "What about your NYC ART entry? T-minus eleven until submission day. Is that what you and Mr. B were talking about?"

"Sort of."

"So, what's your plan?"

"I don't have one."

"You don't have a plan for the most important thing in our lives?"

"Is it the most important thing in our lives?" As I question it, I already know my answer. An art competition is maybe one of the least important things in my life.

Theo stops and tugs my backpack strap to stop me, too.

"Excuse me, but are you in there, Georgia Rosenbloom?" He uses his deeper, stronger Theo-Dare voice. "Who's replaced Super G with this person who doesn't seem to care?"

"I care—just, maybe about different things. I was actually telling Mr. B that I'm not going to enter." I cross my arms over my chest. Challenging

Theo to try to change my mind.

"What? How could you not enter? That's the craziest thing you ever said!"

"I just don't want to."

"But this was our plan. To win together. To have our work hang in the Met together. It won't be the same for me if you're not in it!"

"Guess what—this isn't about you. I'm just feeling like, NYC ART isn't everything."

Theo winces, like I've hurt him with my words. He puts on his deepest Theo-Dare voice: "NYC ART is everything to Super G. Super G must enter!"

"What about *life*, Theo? NYC ART is not real life."

"It is to me," Theo says, in his hoarse, cracking regular voice. "And I thought it was to you, too."

"Well, it's not. I have other things going on, and too bad if you don't get it."

"You're not acting like yourself these days, G. Come back to me when you're ready." He turns from the table we usually sit at for science and finds a seat across the room. Like he can't get far enough away from me.

Upsetting Theo feels like the itch of a mosquito bite I know I shouldn't scratch. I have a twinge of guilt, but I can't turn the clock back eight minutes and erase the conversation we just had.

I think about Frida Kahlo saying she knows herself best. Why don't I know myself best? Do most people feel like they do?

I used to think Dad and Theo knew me best. Better than I knew myself.

But I'm starting to think Theo doesn't get me anymore. And if Dad were to see me now, I'm not even sure that he would still know me.

It's a relief when Dr. Anders rings the handbell on her desk for attention. She turns off the lights and tells us to close our eyes as she describes the moon. She tells us that while the light and heat that come from the sun make life on Earth possible, the moon is a dead world.

"The moon has no atmosphere," she says. "And

the moon's gravitational pull is much weaker than Earth's. Imagine yourself on the moon. You'd weigh one-sixth of what you weigh on Earth. The moon is soundless, and the sky always appears black. So, everyone, stay quiet, eyes closed, and imagine yourselves weightless, leaping and bounding off the rocky surface of the moon, total silence, total darkness."

I want to be in that dark, soundless world, where there wouldn't be different people's voices pulling me in different directions. No choosing between Harper and Theo. Art and Life.

On the moon the only voice I'd listen to is my own. Weightless and free.

"Some of you might've heard of Eugene Cernan," Dr. Anders says, breaking the mood.

My eyes open. The lights are bright again, and everyone else's eyes are already open. Startled, I make eye contact with Dr. Anders, who gives me a reassuring smile.

An image is up on the whiteboard of an

astronaut in a space suit standing on the moon next to an American flag. You can't see his face under the shiny reflective face mask of his helmet, but you can imagine how he feels.

"Eugene Cernan was the last astronaut to walk on the moon. When he died, not so long ago, he left behind a very strong legacy. Not just in his footprints, which will always remain on the moon's surface. He also wrote his daughter's initials in the lunar dust."

That makes me think how Dad left my image in his drawings.

If Dad had been the last man to walk on the moon, he could've made his drawing of me in lunar dust.

And if I were the first girl on the moon, I wonder what mark I'd leave.

If any.

eleven

The world seems distorted through the windows of Harper's silver SUV on the way to her house after school on Friday. Like a painting by Bridget Riley, whose wavy lines ripple in an optical illusion. Dizzying.

Which is how I feel—dizzy, like I'm playing the role of another girl, pretending to be me. The real me would've found Theo after school to make up with him. But instead, the girl I'm playing jumped into her new friend's chauffeur-driven car for a meeting about designing Valentine's Day cards.

For now it's just Harper and me. Chloe and Violet are joining after soccer practice.

The car crosses through Central Park to the Upper East Side. It turns right on Fifth Avenue, left onto a side street, and pulls to a stop in front of a mansion. Literally. A large stone mansion with an iron fence and gates in front.

Harper thanks her driver, who hops out to open the door for us.

Maybe this isn't her house. Maybe she lives in the apartment building next door. But Harper marches straight up to the security keypad on the gate and punches in a series of numbers. It clicks and swings open.

"Wow," I can't help saying.

"Yeah, in LA it was a lot less strange to have a super-huge house." I follow Harper up the steps, through a set of wooden doors, followed by glass doors, into a soaring entryway. "I told my parents to get a regular apartment, but they couldn't find anything big enough for five kids."

There is no smell of urine. No sound of crazy Shih Tzus barking. Instead, I get a whiff of citrus cleaning spray mixed with a pine-forest candle scent and fresh flowers on the console table. The house is pin-drop silent. I'm scared to breath too loud or walk across the marble floor with my dirty boots.

A man in a suit sits at a desk in the entryway. He smiles and nods hello to us but gives me a look like he's making sure I'm not a criminal trying to rob the place. It's just like an adventure for Theo-Dare and Super G—the mansion in Theo's latest story. Only G isn't so super without Theo-Dare.

"Hey," Harper says. "This is my friend, Georgia."

The man gives me a nod of approval. "Welcome." He's no Mrs. Velandry.

"Security. My parents are paranoid about living in the city," Harper whispers to me as we pass through the foyer. I clench my jaw to keep myself from gawking at the art on the walls. I spot some of Dad's favorite artists: El Anatsui, Sean Scully,

Vija Celmins, and a huge painting by Mark Rothko. Blue, yellow, and orange forms of color floating on a canvas.

Dad would've loved it here. He used to take me to museums and galleries around the city and to visit artist friends in their studios. He said art was his religion. "You can worship in front of a Rothko just as easily as in a temple." He taught me how to be still, how to look.

Harper barely glances at the Rothko she lives with every day.

"You've seriously got a Rothko?"

"Yup. My dad's dad was an art collector. He bought a lot of these before they became famous. And now my parents collect, too. Pretty cool, I guess."

"Where're my dad's paintings?"

"Oh, yeah. We should take the stairs. C'mon."

I follow her up the curving wide staircase. I catch a sliver of vibrant green as we get to the second floor.

Charcoal on Green. One of Dad's series of Bird paintings. An abstract image of a pigeon on the grass in Central Park.

"Nice, right? I'm no expert, but this is one of my favorites. Mom loves how it picks up the green of the chairs."

That's how most people buy art. They want something that fits their decoration. But Dad's art is more than just decoration. The Bird series is about color and the experience of Central Park—the contrast between city life and nature. I can feel myself walking through the park with him, watching the pigeons peck around for food in the grass.

I want to go up to the painting, to run my fingers along the visible brushstrokes. Sometimes Dad even used his fingers or a nail to get a stroke just right. If I focus hard enough, I can hear him humming as he worked.

"Let's go to my room." Harper brings me back to the present.

I'd prefer to be alone forever with this painting.

But she wouldn't get it.

"What about his other painting? My mom also said you have *Bird in the Tree*?"

"*Bird*—what?" Harper frowns, unsure. "Um, I don't know. We'll have to ask my mom."

We walk up a few more flights of stairs and I keep my eyes peeled, but I don't see any asterisms. It's not the kind of painting you can miss. On the fourth floor, we step into a huge den area with a wall of desks and bookshelves. A boy younger than us sits at one of the desks, headphones on, hooked up to a computer.

"My brother," Harper says. "Ignore him."

One of the doors opens into Harper's room. All white walls and light wood furniture. No clutter or traces of toys, like the LEGO sets on my bookshelves. There's a framed print that looks like a Matisse paper collage and a few shelves filled with books.

Photographs fight for space on the bulletin board above her desk, but they're sophisticated and cool, not like my childish, out-of-focus Polaroids: smiling, tanned Harper on the beach in a bikini, surrounded by other smiling, tanned bikini girls, hair bleached by the sun. I can't picture myself fitting into the never-ending party that her life seems to be in these photos.

"Do you miss LA?" I ask.

"I miss my friends. Chloe and Violet are great—and you, of course. But there's nothing like the people you've grown up with. Like you and Teddy—so lucky to have each other."

She means Theo. But I don't correct her. "Why'd your parents move here, anyway?"

"Work. Why else? It didn't occur to them that moving five kids from the only home they'd ever had to this cold, dark city might not be the best idea. But here we are." She shrugs.

I never would've guessed that she isn't happy about living here. She always seems cheerful at school, like every day is the greatest day of her life.

"It's not so bad here. When it gets warmer, you'll see."

"In LA today it's seventy-five and sunny." She

flashes the weather app on her phone, which pings with a text. "My mom. Let me just tell her we're here. She wanted to meet you."

Within a minute there's a knock, and Harper opens the door to a woman holding a baby on her hip. She looks like an adult version of Harper, with darker brown skin and darker hair that hangs in glamorous styled waves. She's even dressed stylish, in frayed jeans and a shirt with ruffles on the shoulders. She'd *never* be friends with my and Theo's moms, with their pulled-back hair and glasses and boring clothes.

"You must be Georgia Rosenbloom!" Mrs. Willis takes my hand in hers and squeezes, looking at me like she's meeting someone famous. "I couldn't believe it when Harper told me you two were in the same class. We're *such* big fans of your father; you can't even imagine. Did you see the painting? *Charcoal on Green?* Doesn't it look great with those green chairs?" And with the greenness of Harper's mom. I see that leaf green color all over her. Maybe that's why she was drawn to the painting.

"Mom!" Harper interrupts her.

"Oops." Harper's mom pulls her hand away to cover a giggle. "I wasn't supposed to say all that. But it's true! I just can't help myself."

"Thanks," I mumble. I'm all too used to people telling me how much they love my dad when they don't mean *him*; they mean his art.

"It makes the art more meaningful when we have a personal connection to the artist," she continues, while Harper plays peek-a-boo with her baby sister. "I bet you were even there watching while your dad painted it. Wasn't his studio in your home?"

I nod, like we're talking about some other girl, some other artist. Not *me,* not *my* dad, not *my* home. "I was young when he was working on the Birds. I think he finished the last one when I was six or seven. But I sort of remember." My cheeks flush.

"Mom, please," Harper says. "You're totally embarrassing her!"

"Sorry! We're just so excited for the Met show.

We'll be sad to part with our paintings for it—they're picking them up any day now." She takes a quick glance at her watch.

"My mom said you also have an asterism painting—*Bird in the Tree*?"

"Oh, yes. That's the best. Simply the best. So good that Harper's dad wanted it all for himself. It's in his office."

"And no one's allowed in Dad's office without permission," Harper says, like she's repeating a rule she's heard one too many times.

"Where's his office?" I ask, imagining a midtown skyscraper. "Maybe I can see it there one day?"

"Upstairs—his *home* office," Harper says.

"I give you permission, if you'd like to see it now?" Harper's mom offers.

But just then the intercom buzzes—the security guy announcing that Chloe and Violet are here.

"Have your meeting. I'll show you after." Harper's mom bounces the baby, making her gurgle on the way out.

"Ugh, I'm so sorry," Harper says after her mom closes the door. "I told her not to make a big deal about your dad or anything. All the time we lived in LA, my parents couldn't care less if some celebrity sat down at the table next to us. They were cool. But they're ridiculously starstruck around the art world. I mean, he was just your dad, right?"

"Yeah, it's complicated." No matter what I tell myself about Hank Rosenbloom being just my dad, there's always that other side of who he was. The part that's harder to explain.

Chloe and Violet saunter in, sweaty and smelly from soccer practice; they know where to put their backpacks and jackets, like they're used to hanging out here. They chatter away about soccer. How Lexie hogs the ball, Ella is a useless goalie, and the coach picks on Violet for not trying harder.

I yawn, and even Harper seems bored by all the soccer talk. She calls the Valentine's Day charity card meeting to order, and I take out my sketchbook. I'm grounded by the coolness of the plastic cover, the firmness of the cardboard back, the pencil in my hand.

"Let's brainstorm!" she says.

We come up with four different designs. One is easy and graphic: *Happy V-Day*, written in bubble letters with doodles of flowers and hearts and candies. Another is funny: Principal Lewes as a cartoon cupid, with a speech bubble saying "Be Mine." For the third, we decide on a boy and a girl drawn from the back view, holding hands.

For the last design, Harper suggests the unicorn-mermaid creature I was drawing in art class.

"You mean the mixed-up animal?" I ask.

Chloe and Violet look at me like I'm speaking a foreign language. Which I kind of am, with them. The mixed-up animal doesn't have a place in this room, where everything is what it seems; nothing is mixed up at all. Except for me.

"Yeah, it was so pretty." Harper gives an encouraging smile.

I don't want to disappoint Harper, but I can't share

my mixed-up animals. "I'm not sure that one works for Valentine's Day. I'll come up with something else. Something cuter, like a puppy or teddy bear holding a heart." Or a bearded dragon. Krypto.

A midnight swirl flashes disappointment across Harper's face, but then she goes back to her usual cheerful marigold. "Great! Sounds like we're all set." She claps her hands together. "Georgia, can you have them all ready by the middle of next week?"

"Sure." I calculate in my head that each one will take a few hours to draw.

"Next, let's talk logistics." Harper picks up her phone and reads out a list of tasks. "One: make copies of the cards on cardstock and buy envelopes—that's for Chloe and Violet. Two: make posters to advertise the sale—you can do that, too, right, Georgia?" She enters my name next to that task without even waiting for me to agree.

"Three: set prices and get school approval to set up a table to make sales—I can do that. We'll all help with sales—and with distribution."

"Distribution?" I thought all I had to do was draw the designs.

"Yeah. People will buy cards, write messages, put them in envelopes, and give them back to us to hand out in homeroom on Valentine's Day. That's the whole point." Violet gives me a look like I'm totally missing something.

"We're going to dress up as cupids—it'll be awesome!" Chloe says.

I can feel Harper watching me, to see if I'm on board with dressing up in a silly costume. I shrug. Maybe it'll make everyone forget about my van Gogh fiasco.

Harper claps her hands again. "Okay, then, sounds like we have a plan!"

I take that as a signal the meeting is over and put my sketchbook back in my bag to leave. But Chloe and Violet don't seem like they're going anywhere.

"You're not staying for dinner?" Harper asks me.

If I hadn't already packed my bag and stood up

to go, I'd stay. But with Chloe's and Violet's hard eyes staring into me, making me question whether I even have a right to be here, I shake my head no.

"Really? We ordered extra sushi for you. The best eel-avocado rolls."

Eel, ick. "Sorry," I whisper, hoping this wasn't my one chance.

"Next time," she says, sunny marigold with a genuine smile. Making me believe there will be a next time. "Let me text my mom that you're leaving so she can show you that painting."

"A painting?" Chloe asks.

"Yeah, we own some of Georgia's dad's art."

"Oh, cool." But she's not interested enough to ask to see it.

Harper's mom meets me at the door, this time baby-free, and it's totally awkward saying quick goodbyes to the Mermaids and then walking off with her. It almost would've been less embarrassing to have changed my mind and stayed.

"How'd the meeting go?" she asks.

"Good."

"Harper's got such a big heart," she says as I follow her up the stairs to the top floor. "And she's lucky to have you designing the cards. If you're anywhere near as talented as your dad was . . ."

I bite the inside of my cheek. She doesn't finish her sentence; she doesn't need to. She's saying what everyone always thinks. At least she uses the past tense. *Dad was.*

Harper's mom pushes open the door to what must be Mr. Willis's home office, and for a second I worry that we're interrupting him. But the room is empty and dark. She presses a button and the lights come on. You can't miss it: there, on the wall above his desk, staring right at me—*Bird in the Tree.* The first asterism painting.

I haven't seen this painting since it left our apartment, when Dad sold it. The dark background almost looks midnight blue or deep gray in contrast to the light wood of the wall it hangs on. The stars glow bright and strong, just like I remember. Just like in *Sally in the Stars*, which I can see whenever I visit the Met, and *Man on the Moon*, at the Whitney.

But it's different, seeing an asterism hanging like this, in someone's home. It's unfair that Mr. Willis gets to be with this painting whenever he wants to. Though the way his desk is set up, he sits with his back to it. He probably doesn't even look at it or think about it most of the time. Not like I would, if it was mine.

Then I think, if Dad *had* painted me as the last asterism, that painting probably would've been sold, too. Maybe it's better that he never made it, so I never had to think of myself hanging in someone else's home or out in public, for the world to see. Or maybe Mom wouldn't have sold it, like she's held on to *G in Blue* all these years.

Mrs. Willis interrupts my thoughts. "We're passionate about his art. We wish we could buy another one."

"There aren't many left," I say.

"I know, so sad, so tragic." Now she seems to

look at me for *me*—not just as the daughter of a famous artist. "You must miss him. I can't even imagine."

"That's okay." I pinch myself for apologizing. I hate that my sadness makes people uncomfortable, and that I feel bad for it.

"Oh, honey." She pulls me into a hug that smells the same as Harper, lavender and jasmine. I try to relax into her, but she's all bony, not like my soft and squishy mom. "Georgia, it's so special to meet you, to have you as one of Harper's best friends."

Everything she says washes over me, except for "best friends." I hold on to those words, but I'm not so sure that I'd call Harper the same. When I think of a best friend, all I think of is Theo.

"Do you want a moment alone with the painting? I bet you feel connected to your dad that way, right? By being with his art?"

Somehow Mrs. Willis just seems to get it. But I shake my head no. I don't know what I'd do alone with the painting besides think about how much I miss Dad—and how I wish I could take the painting off the wall to examine it, to see if he drew any sketch marks on the back of the canvas. Which isn't going to happen.

Out on the street in front of Harper's house, it's like I've just come from another planet. Harper's world is not my real life.

I have a sudden longing for *my* world. Which means being cozy at home this weekend with Mom, and Theo and his mom. People who knew Dad as a person, not only as his paintings. People who don't wonder if I'm as talented as him or not. People who simply *know* me—us.

CHAPTER

twelve

The bus ride across town is crowded with commuters and schoolkids, their breath steaming up the windows. Smushed up in the door well, I don't get a seat, but I manage to pull out my phone and text Theo to see if he's home. As the bus winds through Central Park, he still hasn't replied. Maybe he's angrier at me than I realized. He said to come back to him when I was ready. I think I am. But maybe he's not.

By the time we get to my stop on Central Park West, an inky dusk has settled, broken up by the amber glow of the streetlamps. I push my way through the people rushing out of the subway station.

Mrs. Velandry's window is lit up, but she's not watching the entrance. I can see her back as she leans over the kitchen stove, stirring a pot. The mouthwatering scent of sautéing garlic barely hides the pee smell in the vestibule.

I slow down on Theo's landing on my walk upstairs to listen for sounds in his apartment. All I hear is the noise of the TV.

I would knock, but since he hasn't texted back, I'm guessing he still doesn't want to see me.

I turn the key in my door. The lights are off. Mom's out, but I don't remember her telling me she had plans tonight.

I should be excited that she's not home so I can look at Dad's drawing of her on the mantel, but right now I just want to lounge in front of the TV and watch a show that has nothing to do with art.

My phone pings with a voicemail. Mom: "I'm

so sorry, I got caught up at the Met. It's going to be a long weekend here. I'll be home late tonight, so warm up some food, or maybe you can go to Theo's, or ask Mrs. Velandry for something. Love you."

I text Theo again. *Home. Where are you?*

Ten more minutes. Still no reply.

I'm sure Harper never finds herself alone in an empty house. At least she'd always have a sibling there. Or security.

Theo's bedroom light is on across the airshaft. He *never* leaves his light on when he's not home.

I try calling his cell phone, but it goes straight to voice mail.

He's there, ignoring me. This is getting ridiculous. So I call his landline.

His mom, Harriet, picks up. "Hi, Georgie. Everything okay, sweetheart?" It's so good to hear Harriet's voice. "You just calling to check in?"

"Is Theo there?"

"He's been in his room all afternoon. Let me see

what he's up to." She sets down the phone, which muffles her voice as she calls for Theo once, then twice.

Harriet's voice again: "He says he's not feeling well. I'm sorry. You want to come by here anyway, have something to eat with me?"

I wish I could say yes, but if I do, the tears will come out.

So I grunt out a "no, thanks" and hang up.

Theo and I have never been in a fight like this before. Sure, we've squabbled, like siblings, maybe. We argue about silly things, like who left a special marker uncapped and let it dry out or what game to play. But then we get over it. We've never ignored each other like this.

There are a million other things I could do right now. I could get started on my homework for the weekend. I could read. I could paint. But all I can think about is Theo not talking to me and how to fix it.

I could text him a big fat "*SORRY!!!!*" And he

could flash his bedroom light three times to show me that it's okay. And then I could tell him about the last asterism sketch. And we could look together at his drawing of Dad and the drawing of Mom to see if they also have asterism points. Because keeping it to myself is really making my chest ache.

But another part of me is not at all sorry. Not sorry for telling the truth. The truth that just because art is the biggest thing in everyone else's life, doesn't have to mean it's *my* life. The truth that I don't even feel like an artist anymore.

The truth doesn't always make other people happy. Sometimes, it hurts them.

And there's one truth I need to discover—the truth about what Dad meant to paint for the last asterism. The truth that he meant it to be me.

I go back to the living room. Gently, I take the framed drawing of Mom down from the mantel again. I wipe the dust on the glass with the corner of my T-shirt. The lines of this drawing are softer, more detailed, than in the one of me at age ten. Dad was earlier in his career at this point—his work was just taking off, Mom says. He hadn't found his style yet.

I put the frame facedown on the table. The metal latch on the black velvet backing is stiff, and I'm nervous it's going to snap and break. But I'm able to pry it loose. I lift the backing off the frame. There's a piece of cardboard between the backing and the paper. I remove that, too.

But what I'm hoping to find—it's not there.

No sketch, no points of an asterism on the back of this drawing. Nothing. Just a plain old piece of paper.

I resist the urge to throw the whole thing on the floor, let the glass shatter to pieces. How could I think that it'd be so easy to prove that G, *age 10* is a sketch for the last asterism? If it was that obvious, if Dad had drawn an asterism sketch here, wouldn't Mom know about it already?

I fix the frame back up and place it on the mantel. Now when I see Mom's eyes staring out at me from that drawing, I don't feel the love she had when she was looking at Dad, like I used to. Instead, I feel frustration and distance. And I'm not sure where else to look for proof. There are still piles of Dad's drawings on the table, but I'm beginning to think it'd be like finding a needle in a haystack to find anything that matters.

There's nothing good to eat in our fridge, just some raw carrots and string cheese. In the freezer there's a frozen chicken-and-bean burrito. I stick it in the microwave, even though I'm not in the mood. I'd make myself eat eel in a heartbeat if it meant being with the Mermaids instead of here, alone.

The microwave beeps, and the door swings open to a mess that looks like someone threw up in there. It exploded all over. Cleaning up the chunks of bean and cheese makes me want to gag.

But then I'm still hungry. The garlic smells from Mrs. Velandry's apartment waft up to the sixth floor, making my stomach rumble.

A minute later I knock at her door, covering my ears to Olive's sharp barking. It's worth it to snuggle Royal and get a hot meal.

After turning all the locks, Mrs. Velandry greets me with a wide smile on her wrinkled face, in her favorite red-and-white-checked apron, a wooden spoon in one hand and a rainbow pot holder I made for her in the other hand.

"Come in! I'm just stirring up a big pot of your favorite." She gestures for me to have a seat with her spoon, which is dripping green soup onto the floor. Olive slurps it up eagerly. Pea soup sounds yucky and the idea of it kind of is, but nothing is as delicious as Mrs. Velandry's pea soup. Except maybe for her zucchini bread.

The Velandrys didn't have any children, and I don't really have any grandparents. Dad's parents died before I was born, and Mom's parents live in western Canada and we rarely see them. Mrs. Velandry always says she has the dogs instead.

If it's true that owners begin to look like their

dogs, then that's certainly the case with Mrs. Velandry and her Shih Tzus—her face has their smushed-in sweetness and big, round eyes. She's cozy, too, in her hand-knitted cardigans. Mauve, today. That's how I'd paint Mrs. Velandry—in an elegant mauve. Pinkish purple with overtones of gray.

Royal and Olive run circles around my feet. Royal sniffs at my boots and jumps up on my legs with his sharp little paws.

Two jumps, then he stretches out on the floor as if he's spent enough energy for one evening. I lean down to stroke his fuzzy back, the smooth roundness of his head and velvety ears. He nuzzles into my hand.

Olive keeps her distance and barks, as if telling me to mind my own business. Which is strange, because usually she stops when she sees it's only me.

"That's enough!" Mrs. Velandry shouts. She gives the soup a firm stir, and slices homemade brown bread to melt cheddar on top.

Olive doesn't listen to her, either, but eventually

she gets bored of barking. She gives a few half-hearted harrumphs, then pads over to the faded corduroy dog bed and curls up to snooze.

I give Royal a few kisses and put him down on the bed to snuggle with Olive.

"Those dogs." Mrs. Velandry *tsks* as she places a thick bowl of soup and a plate of grilled cheese on the table in front of me. "Shih Tzus are not supposed to be barkers. Don't know what went wrong with Olive."

I laugh. "But Royal loves her, doesn't he?"

"Oh, yes. They remind me of you and Theo. Two peas in a pod. No pun intended."

I give her a confused look, and then realize she means the pea soup.

I smile and dip the corner of the grilled cheese into the soup. That first bite is heaven.

"Where is he these days, your other half?" she asks.

I guess she's noticed us coming home from school without each other.

"Busy with stuff."

"He's a good kid, that Theo," she says as she prepares the dogs' kibble and sets their food bowls down, then comes to sit across from me at the table. "Reminds me of your dad, in a way. How they look at the world. You can see it in his face, that dreamy quality. Something more is going on behind there than meets the eye. That thing that makes them artists."

The grilled cheese suddenly feels rubbery and thick in my throat. The soup, sour. Theo reminds her of *my* dad—but what about me? Don't *I* have that dreamy artist quality, too? But I don't want to have to ask.

"Did he ever used to talk to you about his art?" I ask instead. Because maybe she'll be able to tell me something useful.

"Not directly—but I knew he was always thinking about it. You could be having an everyday conversation with him about the weather, and you knew that in another part of his mind, he was thinking about his work."

I nod. I remember how I'd get frustrated with him when I'd be telling him a story and he'd tell me to hold on while he sketched or jotted down an idea. But maybe that's what made him a real artist.

"You were probably too young to remember how he used to walk Royal and Olive in the park, pushing you for a nap in the stroller. For hours. Those dogs would sleep the rest of the day after those walks."

I don't remember, but I look at Royal, gobbling up his food, and wonder if he does.

"One time he came back—you were still asleep in the stroller—and he was practically manic. He told me he'd gotten the best idea for a series of paintings, from bird-watching. Blue jays, cardinals, pigeons, robins . . ."

The Bird series. Dad did three others in addition to *Charcoal on Green*, which I just saw at Harper's house: *Red on White*, the winter painting of the cardinal in the snow; *Brown on Pink*, the spring painting of a robin perched on a branch of cherry blossoms; and *Blue on Yellow*, a blue jay in the yellow autumn leaves of a tree.

Mrs. Velandry continues: "He left you sleeping in the stroller and took out his sketchbook and a pencil, and sat right here—where you're sitting. Yes, in that very seat. He sketched out the ideas, the whole series, right then and there."

A chill runs through me.

"He even gave me those drawings. After he worked out the idea upstairs over the next few months. He wanted me to have them as a thank-you."

"Where are they now?" My brain is ticking— maybe, on the back of one of those bird drawings, he made asterism points that would later become *Bird in the Tree*—the asterism painting in Harper's dad's office.

"Gosh, you see what a mess it is here?" Mrs. Velandry waves at her overflowing desk and bookshelves. "I'll look for them. I really should keep things like that in a safer place. They could be valuable, right?"

I nod. "Does my mom know about them? I bet they'd be useful for her exhibit."

"Not sure that she does." Mrs. Velandry frowns in realization. "I didn't think of that. I'll tell you if I can find them."

"What about the asterism paintings?" I ask. Maybe she knows something about them, too. Maybe she can tell me something that will show how I might've inspired him to paint the stars, not just Theo.

"Ah, he loved looking at the stars. When your dad first rented the apartment, it was all about the outdoor space. He liked that it had the little balcony for his telescope. Can you believe, he even got me out there once!" She gives a wistful look. "You still use it, I hope?"

"Actually, we can't find our key." I cross my fingers. "Do you have another one?"

"That's a shame. Let me check." She uses the master key from her giant keyring to unlock the metal wall cabinet that stores all the building keys. She scans the rows of hooks.

"Here it is." She pulls the little key off the hook and holds it in her hand an extra few beats, as if deciding whether to give it to me. "It's my only one. Tell you what. I'll get a copy made and then give it to your mom. It's too cold outside anyway, these days, for stargazing."

I don't want her to give Mom the key—she's already misplaced our current one, and who knows if I'll ever see the new one. "But you know Mom's so busy. I'll come get it for her." I think of a reason, fast. "Also, it has something to do with a special surprise I want to make for her."

Mrs. Velandry falls for it. "Deal. As long as you promise no nonsense monkey business, you hear me?" She wags a stubby finger in my face.

I stifle a giggle. She's referring to the time that Theo tried to make a rope ladder from his room to my room. Mrs. Velandry ended up having to call the fire department to rescue him when he got too petrified on his windowsill even to turn himself around and go back into his room. No one besides me was impressed.

"Promise." I smile.

But Mrs. Velandry's attention has shifted to Royal, who's stopped eating. He coughs and shudders and collapses onto his back.

"Royal!" Mrs. Velandry cries, sinking to her knees next to the dog, whose whole body is trembling. "He's having a seizure."

I freeze, watching what I think is the end of Royal's life. *No.* It can't happen this way—Royal was Dad's. We can't lose him now. Not like this.

Mrs. Velandry places her hand on Royal's belly, and after what seems like forever, the convulsing stops. He rights himself, shakes his head, and hobbles to his bed, leaving behind a small puddle of pee.

"Oh, my poor baby." Mrs. Velandry rubs Royal's back. "He doesn't want to eat after a seizure. They're becoming more frequent."

Olive glances at her brother and then puts her

face back in the bowl to finish all the food. Maybe that's why her stomach is almost touching the ground.

I've completely lost my appetite for pea soup and grilled cheese.

"What can we do to help him?" I ask.

"Oh, doll . . . The vet says there's not much we can do at this point, given his age. My poor, poor boy."

My throat is tight, like I'm choking on the tears I'm holding in. Royal is seventeen, which I know is super old for a dog, and his health isn't great. But that doesn't mean I'm ready to lose him.

I sit on the floor next to his bed as Mrs. Velandry cleans up his accident. He seems so delicate now, like a sack of old bones. I'm afraid to lift him into my lap, worried I might hurt him. But then, maybe being held will comfort him. He gives a soft moan of contentment as I pick him up and he molds himself into my lap.

We sit on the floor like that for a long time,

watching *The Sound of Music*, which is showing on TV. I might've even fallen asleep for a bit, curled up with Royal in my lap.

Until the doorbell rings, and Mom is there to bring me home. I stretch and rub my eyes, and reluctantly put Royal back on his bed, with Olive.

Hoping this won't be the last time I see him.

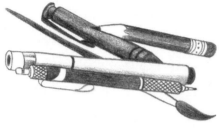

thirteen

Saturday morning I'm heavy with dread from a nightmare that I was walking Royal and he slipped out of his collar and darted into the street. I wake up just as I try to grab him, and then remember the reality, which isn't much better.

I distract myself by going through some of Dad's papers with Mom. His sketchbooks from when he was my age. Things like art class assignments: bowls of fruit, landscapes, people. I study those sketches for signs that one day he'd be a great artist. But all I see is the working and reworking of lines and angles, as he drew and erased and drew again to get something just right.

I hear his voice saying one of his favorite phrases about art: "Practice makes perfect." I never got the chance to ask him what it means if you keep practicing and only get worse—not better. Nowhere close to perfect. Is there such a thing as *perfect* in art, anyway? How do you know when you've gotten to it? And, what if you decide that you can't reach it, so you just stop trying?

Mom opens an accordion portfolio and pulls out a stack of papers. I see her face flush, and she tries to stuff them back in before I can see.

"What?" I ask, pulling on her arm. "What is it?"

"Oh, nothing important," she says. "Just some drawings from around when we first met."

Now I *need* to know. I wrestle the portfolio from her hands; she doesn't put up much of a fight. I pull out the pages and see they're all sketches of a woman. *Mom*, is my first thought. I flip to the back of each page as I look quickly, knowing Mom is uncomfortable, just to see if maybe there are some asterism points on any of these.

And then I see that one of them is nude. It's not super detailed or anything gross, but still—I do *not* want to see. "Ew!" I shove the pages back toward Mom.

She smiles. "They're not all me," she says, coyly. "And besides, nude figure drawing is key to artistic training—I bet you'll do it too, in a few years."

"This is way too much information." I put my hands over my eyes as she giggles. But I kind of like the sound of that giggle—one I haven't heard much in the last two years.

Mom gets her workbag together to head over to the Met for the rest of the day. We plan for me to meet her there for lunch after I go to the stationery store to get a new marker set for the Valentine's Day card designs.

But in the lobby, we hear crying from Mrs. Velandry's apartment.

Royal. I tell Mom what happened last night.

"Oh, my." Mom looks at me with worry, glances

at her watch. She's going to be late to work and risk her eyes getting itchy and watery from the dogs, but she knocks on the door anyway.

"Mrs. Velandry," she calls, "everything okay?"

The crying stops, and the sound of footsteps, punctuated by the thump of her cane, approaches the door. She turns the locks.

"Oh, Georgia and Sally, you're so kind to check on me."

"Of course." Mom tries to peek over Mrs. Velandry's shoulder, to see what's going on. "How's Royal?"

"He's at the vet," Mrs. Velandry says, even as tears drip down her face.

I realize one thing is different, coming into Mrs. Velandry's apartment. Quiet.

"What about Olive?" I ask.

Mrs. Velandry begins sobbing again. Heavy, gasping sobs. Mom reaches out to put her arms around her, to walk her to a seat at her kitchen table.

That's when I see Olive, curled up quiet as a

stuffed animal on the dog bed in the corner. Her eyes are open and moving back and forth, like she's watching us and listening, but she's too sad to make her usual noise without her brother. Her best friend. What if, maybe, all these years, she's barked not to annoy us, but to protect Royal?

Mrs. Velandry tells us how she went to sleep, thinking Royal was okay, that it was just another seizure. But this morning he refused to eat breakfast. So she called the vet, who said she had to bring him in. It's not easy for Mrs. Velandry to go out, but she had to, for Royal.

"The vet is keeping him there for observation and hydration overnight," she tells us. "He's on an IV. But they say his stomach is full of tumors, and if they can't get him to eat . . . Oh, it's going to be tough, my dears. Very tough."

Mom's eyes are teary—I think because she's crying, not just from allergies. I want to run over to the vet's office right now, to tell them to let Royal go, to bring him home in my arms and nurse him back to health. I don't ever want to lose him.

"We have to do what's right for him," Mrs. Velandry says, as if she reads my thoughts. "Can't let him suffer."

I nod, knowing she's right, and try to focus on poor Olive. I wonder if she'll ever recover from losing Royal. Or if, like me, she'll stop working like she's supposed to. She'll stop knowing how to be the dog she was before.

Mom checks her phone; her eyes are getting redder. "I have to get to work now, but please, let me know how Royal is doing. You shouldn't be alone for this," she tells Mrs. Velandry. "I'll come with you, tomorrow."

"Me, too," I say.

They exchange a look. At first I think Mom is going to say no, that I can't come. But then, slowly, she nods. "Okay," she says. "It'll be tough, but I respect if that's what you want."

It's not *really* what I want. What I want is not to lose Royal.

But I know that I have to be brave for him: to say goodbye, to hold him one last time.

Outside, I drink in the relief of the cold air after the staleness of Mrs. Velandry's apartment. Mom pulls me into a strong hug and holds me like that for a long time before I pull away.

She heads toward the bus stop to go across town to the Met, and I walk over to Golden Leaf Stationers, our local art supply shop, trying to clear my head from thinking about Royal. The checkout man, Fareed, keeps a plastic jar of Tootsie Rolls on the counter. He's worked there for thirty years and now owns the store—he bought it after the previous owner retired.

"Miss Georgia. Long time, no see!"

"Hey." I keep the glumness out of my voice. But it shows on my face.

"What's getting you down today? The weather?"

I nod, letting him think the gray skies that signal approaching snow are affecting my mood.

"Where's your buddy?" Fareed asks.

Theo. As if *he* might help me feel better. Theo's more allergic to dogs than Mom is, and he only sees Royal as something that makes his skin break out in hives. I don't think he's touched him once in his life.

"Don't know." I turn to browse the colored marker sets for inspiration.

As I'm deciding between two different sets, a jar of silvery-gray glitter on a nearby shelf catches my eye. It makes me think of something: moondust. That astronaut marking his daughter's initials on the moon.

I snatch up the glitter, four 12″ x 12″ primed wood panels, and a bottle of wood glue, and set them down on the checkout counter, along with a twenty-four-color marker set. An image is swirling in my mind: me, making my mark in the lunar dust, with the glitter as dust. The first girl on the moon.

Even if I'm not going to enter NYC ART, I still have to make a self-portrait for Mr. B's art class.

Fareed rings up these materials. He raises his eyes at the glitter. "Trying something different?"

"Yeah, I guess."

"Different can be good. Different makes you think in new ways, yes?"

"I hope so."

Fareed gets this distant look on his face as he writes down the charge in his book. We have an account here that Mom pays every month.

"Your dad, you know he was one of the kindest men I ever met."

"Really?" I love when people tell stories about Dad, the person. Not just about how much they love his art. I pluck a Tootsie Roll from the jar, unwrap it, and pop it in my mouth. The burst of chocolate brings me back to being here with Dad.

"Yes. Always gentle, always soft-spoken, never a loud word. Some artists, they get all, what's the expression? Worked up. That's it. But not your dad. One time, when you were very little, you knocked a whole shelf of paints over by mistake. Other fathers, they get angry, yell. But not your dad. He laughed, and together we put everything back on the shelf." He shakes his head, that shake people give that means *what a shame he died so young.*

I look for that memory imprinted in my brain somewhere: the clatter of paint cans on the linoleum floor, the clang against the metal shelves, Dad's calm reaction.

But I don't remember.

I want Fareed to keep talking. To tell me more stories. To give me the information I need.

"You be like your dad," Fareed says. "Be the peace. As an artist, and a person."

If only it were so easy.

I nod. "Hey, Fareed, you know my dad's asterism paintings?"

"Of course, yes, those are spectacular."

"Did he buy the paints for them here?"

"I don't think so. We only carry basic acrylics. I don't think he used acrylics for those. Probably used oils from one of the paint stores downtown."

"Well, thanks, anyway." I'm about to leave, not sure what else to ask him, when Fareed clears his throat to speak again. I turn back, hoping for more about Dad, or the asterisms. Instead, he holds out a thin envelope.

"Just one favor, since I haven't seen your mom in a while. Can you give her this?"

"Sure." I take the envelope, which is sealed shut, with Mom's name, Sally Rosenbloom, handwritten on the outside. It has a security lining so I can't see what's inside. But something flat, like a letter. Or a receipt. Or a bill.

The twine handles of the shopping bags, heavy with the wood panels, dig into my wrists, cutting off my circulation as I wonder what it is.

Fareed senses my hesitation. "Don't worry about a thing. Your dad, he was good to me. Just give that to your mom."

The envelope weighs nothing, but my curiosity about what's in it grows heavier and heavier as I walk home. I put it on top of my backpack so I'll remember to bring it with me when I meet Mom for lunch at the Met.

In my room, I clear a space on the desk for my art projects.

First I decide to try playing with the glitter. Moondust.

I set down one of the wood panels and use a silver Sharpie to draw my face in simple lines. Then I squeeze glue along the lines. And sprinkle on the glitter.

But the glue spreads and distorts the lines, and it doesn't look like a portrait of a girl in dust at all. It just looks like curving lines of glitter on wood. The problem is that the glitter has no contour or shading.

Okay, what about another way? I take a second panel and cover the whole thing in glue and glitter. And then use my finger to trace my portrait. I like that idea conceptually—making my mark in the lunar dust—but again, it turns into a mess. I don't even try the third and fourth panels, because my fingers are sticky with gluey glitter.

As I scrub my hands clean in the sink, I'm grateful that at least I have the Valentine's card designs to work on. I know exactly what I need to do for those.

Back at my desk, my hand relaxes and my mind drifts as I work on the letters and patterns for the cards. This is a different kind of art. It doesn't make my brain and heart ache in the same way. I'm not trying to capture some big truth; I'm just trying to make it look pretty.

I sketch the ideas the Mermaids and I planned out. The one that's hardest to get right is the figures of the girl and boy drawn from behind holding hands. I have to think of a specific person when I draw a figure, and the only girl and boy who come to mind are me and Theo.

I decide to change some details, because I don't mean for them to actually be us. So I give Theo black hair, and I give me bronze-brown hair, kind of like Harper's. How much easier to draw myself when I don't have to show my face, when I can change my hair to make it look like someone else's.

Time passes so quickly working on the cards

that before I know it, I need to leave to meet Mom for lunch. I finish up my work and take my folder of card sketches with me in case I get inspired to work on them at the Met.

The envelope from Fareed stares up at me from on top of my backpack. He gave it to me, so it can't be *that* private. I should give it straight to Mom, but I need to know what it is. Maybe something about Dad. What if Dad gave Fareed a drawing—an asterism sketch? I slide my finger beneath the flap, trying to open it as neatly as possible.

Inside, there's one of Fareed's handwritten bills. The ones that Mom is supposed to pay monthly. This one shows November, December, and January. Three whole months. Stamped in red with a big fat *"UNPAID."*

Could things be that bad? Mom said something the other night about how she's hoping the exhibit will drive up the prices for Dad's art. If it's so bad that she can't even pay the bill for Golden Leaf Stationers, then what?

I put the bill back into the envelope and seal it with a piece of tape.

My heart jitters with everything on my mind— Theo and Harper, NYC ART, Royal, the sketch for the last asterism—and now the Golden Leaf bill, burning in my backpack, like a meteor whizzing within inches of Earth's orbit.

In the lobby, the fake cheerful voices of the TV news echo from inside Mrs. Velandry's apartment. She could use some extra love now. I look through my card design sketches and choose the one that's a dog holding a heart. It looks like a Shih Tzu. Like Royal. I slip it under her door and hope it makes her feel better—like it made me when I drew it— not sadder.

fourteen

The Metropolitan Museum of Art overshadows everything around it, with its gigantic columns and welcoming wide steps. Tourists bundled in puffy coats and winter boots mill along Fifth Avenue, salty smells waft from the pretzel and hot dog carts. The bustle of people continues in the Great Hall. Voices echo off the vaulted ceilings. Arrangements of red-berry branches burst from the giant vases in the wall niches.

I weave through the crowds and flash my membership card to get an admission sticker. Some of the familiar-looking guards nod at me.

The Met was my indoor play space when I was little. We'd go almost every weekend as a family. In Arms and Armor, Dad pretended we were knights and princesses. In the period rooms, I imagined I was exploring a life-sized dollhouse. In the modern art galleries, Dad explained the art and told me stories about the artists.

Now I pass through the medieval galleries, the French period rooms, and into the Petrie Court. The Petrie Court, which sounds kind of gross, like *petri dish*, is actually a glass atrium full of sculptures, overlooking the park. I'm greeted by the sculpture of Perseus, sword out, dangling the head of Medusa. When I was little, I liked to pretend Perseus and all the other sculptures were real people who were temporarily frozen. This makes the whole place kind of creepy.

I slip past the line at the café to find Mom seated at a table by the window, talking on her phone. She ends her call when she sees me.

"That was Harriet. She told me you called last night. She was worried about you. Remember, you can call me, too."

I roll my eyes. Of course Theo's mom told her. They tell each other everything. "You were busy."

"Not too busy to talk to you. I'm always here for you. In fact, Harriet and I decided that what we need is a pizza-and-movie night."

"We just had dinner on Sunday," I say. "Wasn't that enough for this week?"

"Well, Harriet and I want to."

"What about what I want?"

"Why don't you want to, anyway?"

"Because—Theo's angry at me."

"Why?" Mom's all alarmed. The possibilities of what I might've done running through her head.

"Because, I told you. I'm becoming better friends with Harper Willis, and I don't think he gets it."

Mom's face goes from alarmed to understanding. "That's all normal at your age. Friendships change;

people grow. But like I said, you and Theo, we as families, have something special that will never change."

What about, what if, we can't afford to live in our apartment anymore? If Mom can't even pay our Golden Leaf Stationers account, how can she pay our rent, and for school? Maybe I'll have to switch schools, move apartments. What then—would that change how Theo and Harriet feel about us?

I'm about to hand her Fareed's envelope when the server comes over to take our orders. I get my usual, tomato soup with extra cheese sticks. And a Sprite, which Mom doesn't keep at home but I'm allowed to have in restaurants. But then, as the server leaves, I think about the cost of paying extra for a drink.

I hand Mom the envelope. She opens it. Her eyebrows knit together as she looks at it. She sighs and slides it into her bag. "You looked at it, didn't you?"

I'm about to deny it, but instead I nod. I want to

know, anyway. What it means for us.

"This isn't as bad as it looks," she says. "Sometimes I just forget. Things slip my mind these days. So much to take care of, to organize, to stay on top of. But once the exhibit opens, it'll get better. I promise."

I wonder what she means by "get better"—that she'll be able to sell Dad's art for more money? Even, maybe, a drawing like G, *age 10*? Because selling that sounds a whole lot worse to me.

"Sally!" a voice calls as we're finishing up our lunch. A deep, rumbling voice that boomerangs around the gallery and that perfectly fits the tall woman striding toward us. Gray hair cut sharp at her chin, black pants and a fuchsia blouse, and a neck that sticks forward like she's spent too many years examining art.

"Evelyn Capstone?" I whisper to Mom. She nods. Evelyn Capstone is the head curator for the modern art department. Kind of like Mom's boss for the Hank Rosenbloom exhibit. I haven't seen her in a few years. But she's the kind of person who leaves a lasting impression, and Mom talks about her all the time at home. "Evelyn this, and Evelyn that . . ." Mom sees her as a mentor.

I hurry to finish chewing my food and wipe at the crumbs around my mouth.

"Evelyn, so nice for you to come by. You remember Georgia."

"It's been too long. Thrilled to see you." Evelyn extends her red finger-nailed hand to me. Her rings dig into my hand and I try to remember to make eye contact with her as we shake, but I worry that she's noticing the crumbs I missed in the corners of my mouth.

"I'm so enjoying working with your mother on preparing the show. She always says such wonderful things about you. That you're becoming quite the talented artist."

"I guess."

"She might've told you that part of my job is

to judge NYC ART, and I hear you're finally old enough to enter." She looks at me expectantly, as if I should be jumping for joy at this news.

I raise my eyebrows at Mom.

Evelyn tilts her head in confusion. "Didn't you tell me, Sally?"

Mom looks torn, like she doesn't want to admit that the daughter of Hank Rosenbloom isn't bothering to enter.

So I say it for her: "I'm not entering."

Evelyn doesn't hide her surprise. "That's a shame. I bet your mom would've liked to have your first art show at the Met at the same time as your dad's. But artists follow many different paths to success. There isn't just one way."

Now I beam up at her. Someone who understands. I feel a sense of relief for the first time since I've made my decision.

"That's definitely true, but . . ." Mom takes a sip of her water. "Will you join us for coffee or tea?"

"No time today—there are some catalogue

pages I want to review with you. But I'd love to have lunch with you both one day soon—to get to know you better, Georgia."

"Sure." I try to catch Mom's eye. Why would Evelyn want to get to know *me* better? But Mom's clearly pleased that Evelyn is being so kind, so I figure it's one of those things adults say that they don't really mean.

Evelyn waits while Mom pays the check, and we get up from the table. As we walk toward the modern galleries, the ornate marble and fancy details of the sculpture court give way to plain white box rooms.

On the ground floor, we see Georgia O'Keeffe's *Cow Skull: Red, White, and Blue.*

"Really," I whisper to Mom. "This is who you chose to name me after? She painted cows' skulls for fun!"

Evelyn overhears me and laughs. "Would you prefer to be called Jasper or Jackson?" she asks as we pass by Jasper Johns's *White Flag* and Jackson Pollock's *Autumn Rhythm.* I love Jackson's enormous canvas spattered and dripped with black, brown, and white paint. And Jasper's idea of draining an American flag of its familiar color. I get something like a steady drumbeat in my chest when I look at those paintings that I don't get with Georgia's.

We reach the wall where Dad's painting of Mom as an asterism, *Sally in the Stars,* usually hangs.

But it's gone.

There's an empty space and a handwritten slip of paper taped next to the wall label.

"The painting is already down in preparation for the exhibition," Evelyn explains. "It's in my office."

At the door of the modern art department offices, Mom asks if I want to come in for a minute to see it.

I say yes, jumping at the chance.

"I bet it's been a while since you've gotten to look at it without all these other people around,"

Evelyn says, gesturing at the visitors who watch us curiously as Mom swipes her badge on the card reader. It beeps and lights up green, and the door clicks to let us in. The first room is a large open space, with a round table in the center, the walls covered in bookshelves holding the department's reference books.

Mom sets her workbag on the table and starts pulling out folders and papers. Evelyn leads me down a long corridor of offices and cubicles to the office at the very end. The largest one, with a huge window overlooking Central Park. But I don't care about the view, because my eye is drawn directly to *Sally in the Stars*. It's like coming face-to-face with Dad's spirit. The darkness of the background glows, like outer space, and the flecks of white—the stars—flicker on the surface.

I stand before it and realize how different the asterism paintings look depending on where they hang. *Bird in the Tree* looked so stiff and formal hanging on the wall of Mr. Willis's office, in a private place that very few people ever get to see. Here, *Sally in the Stars* seems cozier, propped up on the floor against the wall. Maybe also because it's familiar—I've seen it so many times before, whenever I go to the Met—and because it's a portrait of Mom. All those things make it more personal.

So personal, that it's okay for me to touch.

While Evelyn is busy at her desk, checking e-mails on her computer, I reach out and curl my fingers behind the rough canvas, gently pulling it away from the wall toward me.

I know better than this. I know I shouldn't touch it. But I need to. I need to see if there's anything there. This painting is finished—there's a better chance that Dad might've actually drawn asterism points on the back. Evelyn seems too caught up in her e-mails to notice what I'm doing.

I get a quick peek at the back just as Evelyn shouts, "Georgia!"

I snap to attention.

"No touching the art! Not even in my office," she says.

"Oops, sorry." I carefully lean the canvas back into place.

But I got what I needed. There were marks on the back! All I had time to take in was that they were more than pencil marks—darker, like charcoal. Charcoal is denser and would leave a stronger mark. So it makes sense that Dad would've used it, not pencil, to sketch on the back of a canvas.

"Can I take a picture of the painting on my phone?" I ask.

"Sure. Same rules as for the public—no flash."

I snap a few because now I have an idea. I can hold up the photo of the painting next to that drawing of Mom on the mantel, at least to see if the points Dad painted would correspond to the lines of the drawing.

I give Mom an unexpected kiss as I let myself out of the offices, one step closer to proving that my drawing is Dad's sketch for the last asterism.

On my way out of the museum, I decide to pay a visit to one particular painting. I push through the doors into the galleries of European paintings. These paintings are calm and soothing compared to the modern paintings, where the artists are trying to break through the canvas—tear things apart to make a statement.

The old master portraits gaze down on me, like they're full of reassurance: "Don't worry," they'd say. "It'll all be okay in the end. Everything works out for the best," or something like that. I'd like to go up to each one and have a conversation, listen to their stories, hear how they came to have their portraits painted.

And there he is.

Rembrandt.

His forehead is wrinkled, and he looks at me with an expression of truth on his face. Like Mr. B pointed out to us, his hat slants on his head, casting one eye more in shadow. That's the eye that looks hazier, less direct. The other eye is brighter, more focused.

I let my vision blur and try to transpose Dad's face onto Rembrandt's. Dad, before he was sick.

I try to picture what color I'd use to paint him. But all I can see is black and white. It's like Jasper Johns's American flag—every last trace of color has drained from my memories of Dad.

fifteen

At home I hold up the image of *Sally in the Stars* on my phone next to the drawing of Mom on the mantel, but any which way I turn it, I can't make the points line up. Which double confirms that Dad didn't use this drawing of Mom as a sketch for the painting.

But I did see marks on the back of the canvas; maybe he just made the painting directly from those marks.

And then I think about all those other drawings of her I saw this morning. The ones that made Mom blush, that I didn't finish looking through because I did *not* want to see Mom nude.

I'd make myself finish looking through those drawings of her now, if I could. But the portfolio is gone. I search through the piles on the table twice, but I'm pretty sure Mom stuffed it in her workbag along with other papers she brought to the Met today.

I bite the inside of my cheek and take a quick look around her bedroom, to see if the portfolio is on her desk or floor, somewhere in eyesight. But I don't see it and don't want to go digging.

My stomach roils in disappointment with the feeling that I'm never going to find proof. I go back to my room and set G, *age 10* on my desk. I wish she could talk to me, tell me what she knows. If only I'd glanced up from my book then, while Dad was drawing me, and asked him directly, "Are you going to paint me for the last asterism?" Then I'd *know*.

I open to a fresh page in my sketchbook and

begin copying G, *age 10*. It's comforting, following Dad's lines. Like when I was little and we went to the beach and I followed in the path made by his footsteps, my smaller feet fitting into his larger imprints in the sand.

At first I copy his lines to get myself going. But as my drawing takes shape, I like how it's turning out. It's like Dad's here with me, giving me a drawing lesson.

I'm forgetting the sound of his voice. But now I hear it again, low and gravelly.

"Learn how to control your pencil," he'd say. "That's the key to drawing well. Dark shadows give depth to your drawing. Don't be afraid to deepen the shadows."

Deepen the shadows, deepen the shadows. . . .

I repeat this like a mantra, until his voice becomes my voice. I shade and shade until the pencil point is worn down and needs to be sharpened.

When I'm done, I'm exhausted, like I've been in a trance. The kind of zone Theo gets into, barely aware of time passing. I'm starving and needing a nap *and* buzzing with energy all at once.

I look at the drawing again. It's good. Really good—as a copy of Dad's drawing. But nothing more than a copy.

Then I take a silver paint pen and flip over the page. Without thinking about where Dad made the points on his drawing, I try it for myself. I make asterism points on the back of my copy.

It feels right—that this is how Dad made his asterisms. But my points come out different: One point at the top of my head, another on the tip of my nose. One for each of my hands. One for my shoulder.

That's it. Five. I can't even come up with ten. When I compare it to Dad's version, I see that he chose some points the same and some different. Does that mean he saw me differently than I see myself?

What would Dad say? What would he tell me? I listen for his voice, but I don't hear anything.

Just silence.

And then the door opens and closes. Mom's home.

More footsteps follow and more voices. Theo and Harriet.

Theo. One of the only people who could understand how important *G, age 10* is. Make it real—that I might've found proof. But I'm not ready to share it.

I slip the paper back into my drawer, as deep as it can go.

"We're home!" Mom calls out. "Time to eat!" The smell of fresh pizza makes my stomach rumble.

Theo barely looks up at me when I enter the living room. There are paper plates and an open pizza box on the drafting table. He's already halfway through a slice that he's eating right next to a pile of Dad's work. Oil drips from his pizza onto his plate, just inches away from what could be important papers.

"Don't you think we should clear more space?" I say.

Theo puts down his pizza.

Mom looks at me, surprised. She's the one always telling *me* to be careful not to ruin anything.

"It's okay, Georgia." She gives me a don't-be-rude glare. "Here, have a slice."

"Is there any left? You started without me."

Mom and Harriet exchange a glance.

"Sorry. I called for you to come eat. We're starving."

"You could've waited."

Harriet steps in. "Give her a break, doll. I've never seen this woman work so hard! How about you choose the movie?"

"I don't want to watch a movie." But as I bite into a slice of pizza and the food fills me, I realize I'm grumpy with hunger.

"How about *The Princess Bride*?" Mom suggests.

Even Theo shakes his head at that. "*Indiana Jones?*"

But then it comes to me. The perfect movie

for tonight. *2001: A Space Odyssey*. It'll help me imagine I'm floating up in space. Just where I want to be.

Everyone agrees, and we settle into our usual movie-watching seats and I project myself into the space atmosphere, weightless, defying gravity. The silence and darkness all around.

By the end Theo's fallen asleep, his glasses askew on his nose and drool trailing down his chin, but he pops up as the credits roll.

"Time to get you to bed, sleepyhead." Harriet ruffles his hair.

Usually this is when Theo and I beg to hang out just a little longer. For me to say good night to Krypto, or for him to come look at my latest art projects in my room. Or, when Dad was here, to go out on the balcony and look at the stars.

But not tonight. Tonight I have nothing to show Theo. He wouldn't care about the Valentine's Day cards, and I don't have any art to show him. He knows I don't love Krypto like he does, and Dad's telescope is packed away, the key to the balcony is missing, and no one's looked at the stars in forever.

Still, I kind of wish someone would stop Theo and Harriet from leaving. I walk them to the front door to be polite, but I'm also hoping that someone will speak up. But no one says anything. We wave good night without a word.

Even after the door closes behind them, even when I hear their footsteps walk down the stairs and their front door open, I could still call after them. Run to the edge of the stairs, and say, "Wait! Just one thing!"

But I don't.

I lose that moment—the moment that I could pull Theo back in.

I let him go.

It turns into a weekend of letting go: First Theo. Then Royal.

Sunday mornings are a far cry from how they were when the *New York Times* wrote that profile of

Dad's Sunday routine. And this particular Sunday goes down as one of the worst days of my life.

I don't know what the other worst day would be: not the day Mom and Dad told me he was sick, because I didn't understand what cancer meant that day. Not the day he actually died, because on that day it didn't feel real. Maybe one of the worst days was in the weeks after his funeral, when I came home from school wanting to show him a drawing I'd been working on in art class. But he was gone, and so was his art, and it fully hit me that he wasn't there and never would be again.

On this Sunday we have to say good-bye to Royal. Mom and I go with Mrs. Velandry to the Westside Veterinarian, which is one block from our building. Mrs. Velandry hunches up and shuffles on the walk—I wonder how she managed it by herself yesterday.

The receptionist buzzes us in and gives one of those tight, sorry smiles that I remember from the nurses at Dad's hospital.

Mrs. Velandry clutches my shoulder, digging her fingers in until I want to wiggle away. But I stay by her. Mom supports her with one hand on her back and the other under her elbow. We follow the nurse into an examination room, Mrs. Velandry between us.

It smells like a mix of antiseptic wipes and berry-scented dog shampoo. The vet, with a paper mask over her mouth, carries in Royal. I want to tear that mask from her face, to see her expression as she whispers softly in his ear. He's so still, maybe we've already lost him. But once he's in Mrs. Velandry's arms and hears the sound of her voice, his eyes slit open.

"He hasn't eaten. He's refusing water," the vet says, lifting her mask. "We can try to treat, but once they stop eating and drinking, it usually doesn't help. And the other option . . ."

I don't want to hear anymore. I cover my ears as Mom and Mrs. Velandry ask the vet questions and cuddle Royal, telling him what a good dog he is.

Even Mom, who's holding back her sneezes.

My whole body is frozen stiff and shuddering at the same time. Next it's my turn to hold him. To stroke his velvety soft ears, inhale his potato-chip salty dog scent, feel his sweet little heartbeat and nose, which is dry in a way it shouldn't be. I'm afraid—to hold him, to touch him. But I know I have to. This is my last chance, and if I don't, I'll regret it forever.

"I love you," I whisper in his ear, and I imagine he nuzzles me back in return, even though he's barely able to lift his head.

And then it's time.

Mom and I wait for Mrs. Velandry in the reception area, to let her say her final goodbye in private.

As we leave the vet's, I'm disturbingly weightless, floating free from gravity, spinning out of orbit.

CHAPTER

sixteen

At lunch on Monday, I sit at the cafeteria table with Harper, Chloe, and Violet—the orbit into which I've been pulled. Being in their orbit helps me forget about everything else. Dad, Theo, Royal.

I take out my folder of card designs to show them.

"Oh, they look fabulous!" Harper waves her fingers in the air like she's spreading magic fairy dust. "I love it!"

"Yeah, these are cool." Chloe looks at me with new respect.

CAROLINE GERTLER

"I *love* them!" Violet echoes.

"We're so lucky to have you, Georgia," Harper says. "You can't even imagine. I did this last year in LA, and we didn't have any artists in our grade half as talented as you are. We raised three hundred dollars last year. Let's get to work to beat it this year!"

Violet studies the card design with the girl and boy holding hands. She holds it up, like she's trying to figure something out. "Hey, is this supposed to be you," she points at *me*, "and Theo?"

"Me and Theo?" I say it with all the disgust I can muster.

"Oooh, Georgia, are you and Theo in luh-ooove?" Harper teases in a singsong voice. She leans in to make kissy faces at me. "Is he your *boy*friend?"

"No!" I shout, shooing her away. "Theo's just, like, my best friend—and not even anymore."

"Not what?" a boy's voice asks from behind us.

Theo. I've never burned with embarrassment

around Theo before, but now my cheeks are on fire. I don't know how much he overheard.

"See, look," Chloe says. "She *does* like him! Her face is all red!"

The girls laugh, and Theo stares at the ground, fidgeting with his fingers.

"Join us, Theo," Harper says, pulling him onto half of her chair. He plunks down awkwardly; she slings her arm around him.

Theo's turn to flush. He lets his hair hang over his glasses to try to hide.

"Oh, Harps, you're so weird!" Violet says.

Then Harper lets it all loose in a chicken dance, totally unselfconscious as the whole cafeteria watches her, clapping and laughing—*with* her. If it was anyone else, they'd be getting laughed *at*.

She stops, hands on her thighs, and takes in a deep breath as if she's tired herself out. "Okay, people, the fun is over. My burger is getting cold."

She elbows Theo out of her seat, and he's left chairless. He gives me an angry look as he flicks his hair off his face and walks away, back to his own table. *Our* table.

I should get up, pull Theo over to the side, and apologize. Tell him about Royal. But I'm glued to my chair. And maybe, just maybe, he didn't hear me, anyway.

The Mermaids continue to plan the card sale. Valentine's Day is a week and a half away.

"Can we get Theo to help?" Harper asks. "It'd be good to have a boy, too, don't you think?"

"Don't we want a cooler boy, like Alex or Luca?" Chloe asks.

"Theo's cool," Harper says. "He's an undiscovered gem. Just like Georgia."

I go red again. The idea of me and Theo as "undiscovered" is kind of humiliating, but also makes me feel chosen. Special. Only I'm not so sure that Theo's as excited to be discovered as I am.

In fact, I know he's not. After lunch he waits for me at the door to the cafeteria. "I need to talk to you—in private."

"Uh-oh, someone looks like she's in trouble," Chloe says. Harper gives me a kind smile.

"Better go fix things." Violet bumps my shoulder.

The Mermaids link arms and leave me there.

The fastest way to end the conversation is to start by apologizing.

"Look, Theo, I'm sorry." I begin on our way to our next classes. I try to figure out how to tell him about Royal, how hard everything's been, but he crosses his arms tighter over his chest and interrupts before I can say more.

"That's not a real apology. You don't mean it."

"Theo—I—"

"I don't even know who you are these days, G. Do you mean it—I'm not your best friend?"

Like a fish gasping for air, I open my mouth—to say something, anything, to defend myself.

But Theo goes on. "Fine. It's news to me. I can't make you be my best friend. But it's okay. It's not like you're so great to hang out with anyway. You can't keep using what happened as an excuse to treat people however you want."

His words are worse than a punch in the gut.

I find it in me to stay steady and calm. Like Fareed said, *Be the peace.* "Maybe you see it as an *excuse,* but *what happened* makes me who I am." No point in telling him now about Royal—he'll just accuse me of using it as another excuse. I pick up my pace and leave him behind.

If anyone should understand *what happened,* it's Theo. He was there for it. For all of it.

What happened is that my world as I knew it ended. *What happened* is that I became known as the girl whose father died. *What happened* is that everything broke apart. I became a flat shell of myself, like a cut-paper silhouette.

At least with Harper, who wasn't here then, *what happened* doesn't hang over us all the time like a storm cloud, ready to burst and drench us at any moment. With her, everything isn't about Dad and his art. With her, I can feel almost normal.

☆ ☆ ☆

That afternoon Mrs. Velandry is waiting for me at the window. We wave hello, and she has her door unlocked by the time I enter the lobby. I still can't get used to the quiet. Olive's not barking—it's like she's lost her voice. She thumps her tail, raises her eyes at me from her bed in the corner.

"Thank you for all your support this weekend," Mrs. Velandry says, pulling me into a hug. "That card you drew—it made me smile. And you and your mom being there with us yesterday . . ."

She starts to sob. "Olive is so sad. Maybe you want to walk her sometimes, to lift her spirits?"

I'm not sure I can ever make myself care for Olive like I did for Royal, but she looks up at me with hopeful eyes, and I think maybe I can.

"I could walk her most days after school," I offer. "Four p.m.?"

"That would be great, Georgia. We'd both appreciate it. And before I forget." She reaches into her pocket for something. "This is ready for you."

She hands me a tiny brown envelope with something hard and flat inside.

Right. The key. To our balcony. I can't remember exactly why I wanted it in the first place. But maybe, somehow, it'll feel good. To be out there again. To look through Dad's telescope and see things how he did.

"Remember, you promised: no nonsense. Give this to your mom."

"Sure." I cross my fingers behind my back and run straight up to my apartment.

On the first try, I think it must be the wrong key. The lock is so tight that it takes a few nudges before I can turn it. There's a pop of air when I push open the balcony door.

The wind is stronger up here, six floors above the street. I look out over the roofs of the brownstones across from us. Central Park spreads below like a blanket of brownness, the trees still bare, grass faded dull.

Then I look back in through the windows to

our apartment. The glare of the afternoon sunlight means I have to press my face up against the glass to see anything. From the outside, the living room—Dad's studio—looks cozy and warm. Dad's paintings against the walls, the trestle where his paint supplies are stored, make it seem like he's just stepped out for an errand and he'll be home any minute. I want to stay out here forever, to keep that feeling. But I don't know how much time I have before Mom comes home.

I go inside to get the telescope. I take out the stand and the large scope and the lens from the case and try my best to remember how Dad set it all up. Finally assembled, the telescope's almost as tall as me. I struggle to lift it onto the balcony.

There's one major problem: it's still daylight. Of course, I can't see the stars now. But I don't want to take the whole thing apart and put it back in the case and try to set it up at night. I'd risk waking Mom.

So I drag the telescope against the brick wall, just to the left of the balcony door, where Mom wouldn't see it from inside the apartment. I relock the door and fold up the case and stuff it behind the sofa. And hope that Mom doesn't notice what I've done before I have the chance to go back out there tonight.

I force myself to stay awake until I hear Mom snoring in her room. I throw my puffy coat over my pajamas and slip my bare feet into snow boots before unlocking the balcony door and stepping outside into the clear night.

The crisp, cool air brings me back to those nights with Dad. And Theo—but I don't want to think about him. Not now.

I put my right eye up to the lens. Nothing but darkness. I turn the knob to focus. Still nothing. All a blur. I re-angle the telescope and turn the knob slowly all the way in one direction, and then the other. More nothing. I can't get it to focus. Not the way Dad could, with just a few light touches and adjustments.

A surge of frustration rushes through me and I want to kick the stupid stand over, to shatter the lens, to stomp on that useless piece of metal.

Instead I take a few deep breaths and try again. Slower this time. Until there's a sudden, sharp focus, and I'm actually seeing stars! I have no idea what star, or planet, I'm seeing. But it's something. That bright glow pulses at me, like it's Dad, winking down from the heavens. I pull my face away and close my eyes, slowly, deeply breathing in the quiet night air. I can feel him next to me, like he used to be.

I look back through the viewer, try to focus on another star, but can't seem to find anything else. Rather than get frustrated again, I carefully disassemble the telescope, putting each piece into its section of the case.

Just as I'm about to zip it closed, I feel something stuck in one of the pockets. A piece of paper. An instruction manual, maybe.

No—a folded piece of paper. Thick, like it came from a sketchbook.

I hold my breath as I unfold it. Maybe this is the evidence I need—an asterism sketch.

I glance quickly at the image and then crumple it as tight as I can.

It's only one of our mixed-up animals. I remember making this one: Dad drew the giraffe head, Theo drew the hippo body, and I drew the human feet.

But then I smile, remembering how it was one of those days when Theo couldn't sit still, and he skipped around the room until it was his turn. How fast he sketched his part of the drawing and then told silly knock-knock jokes with Dad while I drew my part. How absurd I thought I was being, making the feet human. But, of course, Theo pointed out that humans are animals, too.

I smooth the paper flat, and even though it's still wrinkled, I put it in the folder in my desk drawer, along with all our other mixed-up animals.

CHAPTER

seventeen

Later that week in art class, Mr. B sets jars of fresh blue paint on the tables. I sink my brush into the liquid blue and enjoy the feeling of dabbing the paper, twirling the brush in circles.

If I were Dad or Theo, the inspiration would start to flow. The act of swirling my brush around on the paper would bring me to that zone.

But all I see on the paper are plain blue circles.

Mr. B comes up behind me to peek at my work. "Interesting," he says, though he sounds disappointed. "But where are you going with it? You need to *feel* the blue. Feel it in your hand, through the brush, onto the page. Make the expression of feeling visible in that color. What are you trying to show here?"

"I'm not sure." My voice cracks, and my hand loses its grip on the brush with every word Mr. B says—every way he tries to make me work harder, dig deeper.

Hearing the wobble in my voice, he relaxes. "That's okay, Georgia. Sometimes we don't always know what our point is when we get started. It takes starting something, trying it, to figure out what you want to say. Speaking of which, any thoughts on NYC ART? Submission day isn't until Monday."

I shake my head.

Even if I did change my mind, I don't have anything to show for it. The lunar dust portrait was a total bust, and the mixed-up animal drawing is too personal and probably wouldn't qualify for the self-portrait theme. And my copy of Dad's drawing with the asterism points on it is pretty much plagiarism.

"Anything I can help you with?"

Could he help if I explain that I found Dad's drawing of me at age ten, and that I think it's a sketch for the last asterism? That it means everything to me, and I want to prove what it is? That I care more about that than about making my own portrait?

He stays a moment longer, to say something else. If only he could find the right thing.

But he moves down the table to the next group of students.

Over the weekend I feel trapped in my aloneness. Theo and I aren't talking. Plus, he's busy with musical rehearsals. I'm not enough of a Mermaid to ask Harper to hang out, and she hasn't asked me. Harriet has another date with the economics professor and Mom's working, so no one's there for Saturday pizza-and-movie night. I take Olive for long walks in the park. She seems to get her voice back—outside, at least, barking at other dogs.

From my room on Sunday afternoon, I see the

light on in Theo's room. Where I'd be working away, perfecting my NYC ART entry, if we weren't in the first big fight of our lives. And if I wanted to enter.

Boredom leads to art. Not to make a competition entry, just to play. And to make the self-portrait I have to do for class anyway. I pull out the third wood panel I bought for my lunar dust portrait idea. This time I think of the human feet from the mixed-up animal drawing I found in Dad's telescope case. Why not draw my self-portrait as a disembodied body part—just my feet? My feet, walking on the moon. Taking steps in the lunar dust.

Again, big fail. The lines of glue look nothing like feet, just blobs of glitter. I'm no better than a little kid doing finger paint and the glitter gets everywhere, under my fingernails and even in my eye when I forget and rub at it by mistake.

The only thing that seems right is Dad's drawing, *G, age 10*. I reach into my desk and pull it out.

The drawing has imprinted itself on my brain.

I've memorized every line, every curve. I could draw it without even looking.

I take out a fresh piece of paper.

But my hand doesn't want to cooperate. My pencil marks are stiff and lifeless on the page.

I draw my face over and over until it looks like a hollow mask of me. Nothing to do with me, at all.

I once read about a guy who draws in his sleep. An artist-sleepwalker. When he's awake, he can't even draw a straight line. But in his sleep, in the middle of the night, he makes art that sells for thousands of dollars. Maybe that could happen to me if I stop trying.

Or maybe I'm losing my ability to draw altogether. That thought freaks me out, but it's also freeing. Like if I can't draw anymore, no one will expect me to be an artist. No one will care if I'm never as good as Dad.

The afternoon passes, and something changes with the light outside. I glance out my window and notice Theo's room is dark. He's turned his light off. I wonder where he's going. I could run out of my apartment to try to bump into him accidentally on purpose. But I don't.

Seconds later there's a knock on my door.

"What, Mom?" I don't even try to hide my irritation. I thought she was working at the Met all day.

The door opens a crack.

"It's me."

Theo. The only person who knows he can walk right in, that we keep our front door unlocked when we're home.

"Oh, hey." I shove Dad's drawing onto a messy pile of papers on my desk. I don't want him to see it.

"What are you working on?"

"Nothing, really. Just playing. I had this idea, but it's kind of awful." I hold out the lunar dust panels for him to see.

He tries to look thoughtful, but I see right through to the negative judgment on his face. His lips are twisted funny, like he's had a spoonful of fish oil. I let out a giggle.

"They suck, don't they?" I say.

He moves his mouth like he's trying to find something nice to say, but he can't. "Yeah, kind of sucky."

It's totally mean and totally true, and breaks the ice between us. We both laugh. An uneasy, not quite *us* laugh. But still, a laugh. Better than silence.

"They're more than sucky, they're horrific! Terrifying. Disturbingly, devastatingly horrid!" I say in a strong Super G voice.

Now we burst into a fit of uncontrollable giggles. Real, true, old-school Theo and Georgia giggles.

Maybe we *can* get over the past couple of weeks and just go back to being us.

"Can I show you my entry?" he asks.

"Sure."

He places a manila folder on my desk and opens it.

I catch a glimpse of a beautifully painted Theo-Dare panel before he snatches it back.

"I'm finished, and I don't have time to make any

changes. So hold the criticisms, please. Too late for that."

"Theo, let me see! I'm sure it's great."

He turns the paper to show me the image. "I would've liked your input earlier, but . . ."

"But, what, Theo? This is amazing! I have nothing to say except congratulations."

And I mean it. The panel is more than just his typical sketch of Theo-Dare in action. He's drawn himself in pencil, as usual, but he's also finished it by going over the lines in black marker and coloring it with gouache. Theo-Dare looks into the distance, one hand raised to his forehead as if shielding his eyes from the sun, the other hand pointing. The speech bubble reads, "If I can reach it, I can do it. . . ."

Theo beams with pride as I take it in. He knows he did it. He's *so* going to get into NYC ART.

"I love how the thought bubble doesn't tell you the whole story, but makes you wonder what's going on."

"Yeah, I wanted it to be open to interpretation.

Like the viewer can imagine their own story into it."

"Totally." And as usual, talking to Theo about art gets my own wheels spinning. "Maybe I was thinking too literally for mine."

"Hey, what about this one?" Theo points to my desk, at the pile where I shoved G, *age 10* in the corner. "This one looks good."

"Oh, that's nothing. Just me doodling away." I take the pile of papers and put them into my desk drawer, where I should've hidden Dad's drawing to begin with.

"Do you want me to help you?" Theo asks softly. "We could work on something now, get your entry ready for tomorrow?"

Theo's offer to help and the word *entry* shut down any spark of inspiration. "I meant it when I said I don't want to enter."

"I just—I guess I understand. But I really don't. Remember how we used to go with your dad to see the exhibition every year? And we'd talk about what it'd be like when it was our turn? When we finally got to enter and have our first real show?" He looks so hopeful, like he can't believe I don't want what he wants. "I can't imagine getting in and you not being in it with me. And think of all we could do with those thousand-dollar checks. We could take an art class together at the Met this summer! How could you *not* want to, G?"

The blood roils in me as Theo talks. Like one of those volcano experiments with baking soda and vinegar bubbling over—all the anger and confusion and upset and everything I've lost. But I bite my cheek and clench the tears in my eyes.

And then he says the one thing that crosses the line.

"Your dad would want you to, G. I know he would."

It all erupts out of me in this moment.

"How do you know what my dad would want?"

"I'm just guessing."

"You don't know! Because you weren't actually his child! Even though you wish you were! He was *my* dad, not yours!"

You'd think that'd make Theo get up and leave. I've said the most hurtful thing I could think of. He just stands there looking upset. But not as upset as he should be.

"Go!" I scream. "Leave!"

Theo doesn't budge.

So I go.

I storm out of my room into the kitchen.

I stare at that framed article on the wall about our Sunday routine—the *old* Sunday routine.

I can't read the words because my eyes are blurry and wet. But I don't want to cry. I haven't cried in so long, and I'm not starting now. My body heaves with misery, with holding it all in.

Theo comes up and gives me a pat on my shoulder, but I elbow him away. "Just leave!"

Too many minutes pass before I hear the door close and he's gone.

Monday is submission day. It comes and goes with no fanfare for me. But not for Theo, who's on his way to getting into his first real art competition. It makes me feel even more distant from him, that he's doing this big thing without me.

I don't even know if he's angry at me or thinks I'm pathetic or what. I guess we're back to not talking, after the way I yelled at him.

In science Dr. Anders asks, "What would happen if the sun disappeared?"

We're supposed to be horrified, but right now, the idea of something catastrophic sounds good to me.

"Would there be utter darkness, chaos, immediate destruction? Or could we go on living somehow?"

"Chaos!" Luca yells out.

"No more sunbathing," Chloe says.

Everyone laughs.

"The good news," Dr. Anders says, "is that the stars would still shine, and electricity would continue to work as long as power lasted. The one thing that would end immediately is photosynthesis, and most small plants would die within days.

"Even worse, the temperature of the Earth would drop one hundred fifty degrees Fahrenheit by the end of the first year. The oceans would freeze over, transforming Earth into an ice world. Most living things would die.

"Earth would keep moving, however. And eventually, if it doesn't collide with any other large bodies in space and explode"—we all groan at that—"it could get drawn into the orbit of another star. Any of the hundred billion stars to choose from."

Dr. Anders makes it sound easy—like the earth could just switch orbits. Our sun explodes—*whoops!*—go find a new star to be the sun.

I get it—how it feels to be the Earth, to lose your sun. Like Dad was my sun that disappeared, and I've been drifting ever since—until I got pulled into the orbit of Valentine's Day cards and cupid costumes. An orbit I'm still not so sure I belong in, but which I don't know how I'd leave, even if I wanted to.

CHAPTER

eighteen

The week leading up to Valentine's Day, the Mermaids set up a table in the school lobby during lunch periods for us to sell cards for two dollars each. Everyone loves the designs, and there's a steady crowd of kids around us handing over bills, writing messages, and addressing envelopes.

Except for Theo. He approaches the table with disdain and studies the card designs like an art critic. I wait for his opinion, even though it makes no difference what he thinks. Sales are going better than expected and we already had to print extras.

"You going to buy one?" Harper flashes her biggest smile.

"Um, no thanks." Theo puts the cards back on the table.

"C'mon, you're not going to send one to me?" She makes a sad face.

Theo *cannot* be falling for this corniness, but he blushes and shakes his head.

"How about for Georgia?" she asks.

He looks at me like he's forgotten who I am. "Maybe tomorrow. I didn't bring any money today."

"Here, choose one on me!" Harper says.

I can tell Theo doesn't want one, but forced to choose, he takes the one with the girl and the boy. Chloe and Violet snicker, but Harper keeps a straight face.

As he walks away, the Mermaids huddle together and chatter about what just happened and who Theo's going to send his card to.

But I keep my eyes on Theo.

Just before he turns the corner, he rips the card in half and throws the pieces into the garbage.

By Thursday morning, Valentine's Day, Harper proudly announces we've made three hundred seventy-five dollars, beating her goal for this year.

"Congratulations, ladies!" Harper waves around the envelope stuffed with cash. "We're the best team."

I've never been part of a team before. It feels good. It even feels like no big deal to put on the ridiculous cupid costumes she bought for us to wear to deliver the cards: red leotards with sparkly tutus, sparkly white wigs, and plastic bows and arrows.

I never thought I'd see the day that I'd be dressed up with the Mermaids, part of their scheme. But under Harper's direction, it works.

We carry tote bags full of cards into each homeroom. I hold the tote while Chloe and Violet pull out the envelopes, and Harper reads the names out loud, and we all take turns prancing around to hand out the envelopes.

After I relax into it, I start to enjoy myself. Dressed up as a cupid, I'm no longer quiet, boring, artist Georgia. I'm cute and fun and pretty, too. Someone who everybody else watches. Like I'm truly one of the Mermaids.

Until I see Theo. Glaring at me from his seat in homeroom. Like he knows this is not who I really am.

So I flip my hair and give a little finger wave as I prance by him to deliver a card.

Theo only gets one card. I wonder who it's from. Not me—I didn't send him one. And he didn't send me one, either. I get three cards, one from each of the Mermaids.

"That was awesome!" Violet says as we gather together, back in our regular clothes, after school. I'm breathless over how well the card deliveries went. But part of me also wonders what's next— what I have to look forward to now that this is over.

Harper has an idea ready. "High fives all around!" She waves the money envelope, fat with cash from the card sales. "Happy Valentine's Day, ladies! Let's celebrate! Shooting Star?"

The girls jump up and down in agreement.

Harper stuffs the money envelope into her backpack. A few loose dollars fall to the floor.

Violet traps them under her foot and leans down to pick them up, missing a dollar.

"Here." I bend down to get it and hand it to her.

"Oh, thanks." She takes it from me like it's a used tissue, as if that one extra dollar doesn't matter. She shoves the bills into her pocket, not bothering to put them into the envelope with the rest of the cash.

I'm light and loose, walking out on the street with the Mermaids, the bright sun giving a cheerful energy even though it's still super cold.

But being in the coffee shop with Harper, Chloe, and Violet is not as fun as it looked from the outside.

Just the opposite. I feel like I need to say something interesting, because they're totally bored and restless, refreshing the feeds on their phones every five seconds. Violet exclaims about a picture someone I don't know posted and starts texting, which makes Chloe's and Harper's phones ping at the same time.

My phone is quiet as usual, and I can't think of anything on it that would get their attention, so I come up with something to say, instead: "Would you rather . . . eat a horse or a rabbit?" Pinching myself for such a ridiculous question.

"Ew!" squeals Violet. "Rabbit, for sure. Isn't that, like, venison?"

"I think deer is venison," I say, grateful that she's running with it and not looking at me like I'm the weirdest person in the world.

"But in France they eat horse, don't they?" Chloe says.

"Hey, I used to ride horses!" Harper protests. "Count me in for rabbit."

"I'm vegetarian," Chloe says. "So I choose neither."

"Cop-out!" Violet says.

"Hey, you can't make me choose something that totally violates my moral principles!" Chloe balls up a napkin and throws it at her.

"Okay, then you're up next," Violet says, tossing the napkin back at her.

Chloe thinks for a few seconds, then asks, "Would you rather vomit all over yourself in front of Principal Lewes or the boy you have a crush on?"

"Principal Lewes!" we all shout at once.

"Can we turn this game to more appealing topics?" Harper asks. "I'm losing my appetite here."

"I've got one," Violet says. "Would you rather have the power to turn invisible or be the most beautiful person in school?"

"Huh?" For Chloe, the choice is clear. "Be the most beautiful, obviously."

"Same," Violet says.

"Invisible," I murmur.

We all turn expectantly to Harper, who I'd bet will agree with Chloe and Violet. But her eyes darken and her marigold color turns mustard-y as she whispers, "Invisible. I'd *love* to be invisible sometimes."

"Really?" I blurt out.

"That's because you're already the most beautiful," Chloe says. "Not a fair question for you."

"No, seriously," Harper says. "I'm not saying I'm so beautiful, but people *do* look at me a lot. For whatever reason. Maybe they're trying to figure out what race I am, or why my family is freaky big with all my siblings running around. Or whatever. But I just always feel like people are looking, like they think they have a right to. Who knows. And all those siblings make us like a traveling circus—they drive me crazy. Always needing something, and my mom totally expects me to be, like, her mother's helper. I'd like to be invisible sometimes. A lot of times."

I nod, understanding the desire to be invisible, but not how it feels to have people look at you all the time or to have a big family. I never thought before how those things could be hard for someone like Harper.

"Oh, c'mon Harper, you *know* you're beautiful,"

Chloe says. "Didn't you get a modeling job offer the other day?"

"That's not the point she's trying to make," I say before I can stop myself. "I don't think she's fishing for compliments."

Harper gives me a smile of understanding; Chloe shakes her head. "Whatever. Harps, I'd switch places with you in a heartbeat."

The server brings over the steaming plate of thick golden French fries. Harper drizzles ketchup in a few spots around the edges, and we dig in.

One thing *is* just like I imagined: the French fries *do* taste better with the Mermaids. And they ordered a chocolate shake. With four straws. It's the most delicious combination ever, even though the server rolls her eyes at four of us sharing one milkshake.

"So who got the most cards today?" Violet asks. They pull out their cards and pile them on the table.

I don't bother taking out my three; I don't have to count to know I lose.

Harper wins with fifteen cards. Violet has nine, and Chloe has eight.

"Not fair," Chloe whines. "I knew you'd win, Harps, and you're still new here."

Violet teases Chloe by holding up her thumb and pointer into an L at her forehead.

"She's not the loser," I pipe up. "I am. I only got three."

They all turn their attention on me. "Aw, poor Georgia," Harper says. "We each sent you a card. What about Theo?"

"Nope. Not even from Theo."

"Did you get a card from Theo?" Chloe asks Harper. "You'd think he'd send it to you after you gave it to him for free."

"Nope. What about you ladies?"

They shrug.

"I wonder who, then," Harper muses.

Only I know that it went into the garbage.

"That's way sad." Violet looks concerned for me. "Is he still mad at you?"

"Maybe."

"But you're, like, best best friends," Chloe says. "How could you not make up?"

"I tried. Sort of. I guess it's . . . complicated."

"We can help!" Harper says. "Let's invite him to your party."

I haven't even been thinking about my birthday, not to mention a party. I'm surprised it's still on Harper's radar.

"I don't know."

"If you don't, I will," she says. "I've never gone ice-skating at Wollman Rink. How about that? With dinner and cake at my house after?"

"Cool!" Violet and Chloe agree.

"Just us girls and Theo," Harper says.

I feel like I've lost my voice.

"But does she know . . ." Violet asks, looking at me. Harper blushes.

"What?" I'm confused.

"Harps, you have to tell her," Chloe says.

Violet's nodding, like they're all in on some secret together.

"I can't!" Harper groans.

"Just say it. Tell her," Chloe eggs her on.

Harper's face is a mix of shame and worry, like she's done something wrong and wants my forgiveness. My pulse gets faster, wondering what's going on here. Maybe this is all some joke they're playing on me.

"It's about Theo," she says. "I think he's kind of cute!"

I'm relieved that it's not about me, but also surprised. "*You* have a crush on Theo?" I ask.

"Maybe." She twists her hair into a long rope and lets it fly out around her. "I had a boyfriend in LA, but the long-distance thing wasn't working for us. Theo's just so nice."

I don't know how to wrap my head around Harper thinking that Theo is cute. The other day she said she thought he was cool, like an undiscovered gem.

But how did she get from gemstones to a crush? They don't go together—Harper and Theo. They're like complementary colors—orange and blue, or red and green—which are actually opposites on the color wheel. The colors that contrast so strongly, they make each other stand out the most. But not necessarily in a clashing, bad way. Maybe, sometimes, being different makes them more interesting.

"I don't know; I just don't see it," Chloe says.

"Yeah, I'll never see him that way," Violet agrees. "I mean, when you've known him since kindergarten and he used to wear his Superman underpants on top of his sweatpants to school."

Even I giggle at that. I'd forgotten Theo used to do that—he thought it looked like a superhero costume. Maybe Harper will back off Theo if her friends don't approve.

"You know he has a pet lizard named Krypto?" I tell them, feeling bad as soon as I put it out there as something more for them to laugh about.

"Seriously, Krypto? What kind of name is that?" Chloe says.

"For Superman's dog." Violet shakes her head. "Yeah, I remember. My little brother's obsessed."

"Mine, too," Harper says. "And don't tell anyone, but I kind of have a thing for reptiles." None of us can tell if she's joking or not, so we all giggle.

"Anyway, I sent him a card," she goes on, with a coy smile. "From 'a secret admirer'!"

Theo's one card. From Harper.

The girls bounce in their seats, plotting ways to deepen the mystery and intrigue around Harper's crush.

Harper notices me being quiet. "You're not mad, are you, Georgia? I mean, you said you don't like him that way."

I shake my head. "No, it's fine." I don't know *what* way I like Theo anymore.

The server drops our check on the table. I pull out my wallet to get my share.

"No worries," Harper says. "We got this."

I don't want them to treat me like I'm a charity case. As I pull out my money, Harper lifts up her backpack, reaches in, and takes out an envelope.

The envelope.

The one with the cash from the card sales.

She takes out a twenty-dollar bill.

"Really, we got it." Harper puts her hand on mine to stop me from putting down my money.

Harper drops the twenty on top of the check and hands it to Violet, who slides out of the booth to go up to the cashier and pay.

I snap my jaw closed.

That money is supposed to go to a charity, for the women's and children's homeless shelter. It is *not* supposed to pay for our French fries and milkshake. "Isn't that the charity money?"

Chloe shrugs. "Yeah. We're just borrowing."

"Think of it as reimbursement. For our expenses. Don't worry, I'll pay it back," Harper says.

I nod. I can tell myself to believe her, even if I don't. Even if it doesn't *feel* right.

Violet comes back to the booth. She leaves the few dollars change from her pocket—the ones that fell on the floor before—on the table as a tip. "Why does everyone look like someone just died here? Oops." She slams her hand over her mouth, looking right at me. "I'm so sorry, Georgia; I didn't mean to say that."

At first it doesn't even occur to me what she's apologizing for.

Harper's puzzled, too.

"You're so insensitive, Vi!" Chloe punches her arm.

Then I realize. I swallow the lump in my throat. It's tight, like I'm not going to be able to get a breath. I bite the inside of my cheek.

"Oh, your dad," Harper says.

"It's okay," I say to reassure them, hating myself the moment I say it for my need to play down my own feelings.

We get up to leave. They're all bubbly and chatty, like nothing happened. But I can't just let it go—the money thing.

When we walk out, the sun has fallen behind the buildings. The forecast is for snow. I can feel it in the flatness of the sky.

"You're not going to tell anyone? About the money? Promise?" Harper looks worried as she whispers to me, away from the other girls.

"Promise," I whisper. I don't know who I'd tell, anyway.

"You're the best." She wraps me in her lavender-jasmine–scented hug and kisses my cheek before sashaying off to climb into her silver SUV with the other girls.

They don't offer me a ride for the few blocks to my house. "See ya tomorrow, Georgia," Harper calls to me out the window. Each step toward home makes my lungs burn with cold. As they drive off, they lower the windows and all the girls wave at me.

I wave back. But my heart is no longer in it. My heart is nowhere.

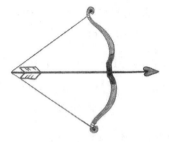

CHAPTER

nineteen

Mom hasn't had a Valentine's date for the past two years, and we all need cheering up right now. The last few years we've done takeout with the Goodwins for Valentine's Day, but Theo hasn't spoken to me since Sunday, and I doubt Mom and Harriet planned anything since Mom's been so busy. I imagine Theo and Harriet downstairs, having their own special dinner, or maybe Harriet's going out with her economics professor.

So after I walk Olive, apologizing to Mrs. Velandry for being late that day, I decide to make a special dinner for Mom. I even invite Mrs. Velandry, who unsurprisingly says she'd rather stay home with Olive.

I set the table with the silver candlesticks from Mom and Dad's wedding, their blue-flowered wedding china, and antique crystal wineglasses which I fill with sparkling water.

The snow starts falling while I put water to boil for pasta and make a simple tomato sauce and a box mix of brownies. Up here, through our windows, the snow is pure and untouched. The apartment smells of garlic and sugar; I light candles to set the mood.

Mom comes in, her hair sparkling with snow, her face red from the cold. She goes from sour and tired to glowing and happy when she sees what I've done. "So romantic!" she says as she takes off her boots and puts on her indoor slippers.

"Will you be my valentine?" I ask her.

"Of course! Always and forever. You're my number one valentine."

"What about Dad?" I ask, leaning back from her. "I thought he was always your number one?" And still is, the way she works so hard to carry on his art, his legacy.

Her face drops a little. "It's a different kind of love. You're both my number ones, in different ways. No one will ever replace your father; you know that." But how is she so sure? What if someday, she wants to find someone new—like Harper maybe taking over Theo's spot as my best friend? Or maybe not, after what she did today.

I pull out Mom's chair for her to sit, and she takes a few bites and tells me how delicious everything tastes. I try to find a way to ask her about what's really on my mind: about people doing things they know they shouldn't. Like Harper using the charity money to pay our bill at Shooting Star. Like me taking G, *age 10* and stashing it in my drawer. But it's easier to follow the line of questioning we're already on, so I ask, "How do you know if you love someone enough to marry them?"

"You mean, like with Dad? Or if I met someone else?"

"I guess, someone else."

She swallows her food. "It takes time to get over a great love like I had with your father. I don't know if I'll ever meet, or want to meet, someone as special to me as he is. But even if I do, that doesn't change the fact that he's your father, and part of you, and us, and his art, forever."

G in Blue glows at us from where it's propped against the wall as we eat our dinner. Lit by candlelight, the blue triangle almost seems alive, moving. Like part of Dad really is here with us. It hasn't gone to the Met yet—but soon. And when it goes, I'll miss him all over again. And I don't even have any real answers, yet, about *G, age 10* and the points on the back.

Maybe it's time to tell Mom, to let her do the work she's trained to do. But that would mean admitting to her what I've done—essentially, stealing one of Dad's drawings. As much as I think I could keep it to be mine, forever, I know that's not right. All of Dad's work, even the quickest sketch, is part of his estate. All of it is potentially valuable. Saleable. Or at least, worthy of being catalogued, archived.

"Mom," I begin as she swirls another bite of pasta on her fork, "do you ever do things that might be wrong, and you're not sure why?"

She pauses with her fork midair. "You mean like a mistake? About what?"

"I mean, like taking something you really wanted, and you thought maybe it was wrong, but maybe it wasn't, and you did it anyway?"

She puts her fork down. "Is this something about you and Theo? Harriet's noticed that you're drifting apart, and I said I thought it better not to push things with you two right now."

Maybe Theo told Harriet how I've been acting. Maybe that's why we're not doing Valentine's dinner with them.

"That's not what I meant. But, yeah, that's something, too."

"You mentioned you're becoming better friends with Harper Willis. Is that coming between you?"

"That's just the thing. It shouldn't. I mean, Harper wants to include Theo, too, but you know how stubborn he is. It's like *he's* forcing me to choose between friends. And she's like a magnet, pulling me away."

Mom nods, smiling. "Ah, charisma. That's how Dad was. Someone who draws you in. I felt it from the moment I met him."

Mom and Dad met when she was a graduate student, finishing her PhD in art history. Dad's career as an artist was taking off. He came to do a lecture for a class where she was a teaching assistant.

"Of course, everyone else felt his warmth, too," she says. "It was obvious from how they all wanted to get close to him. Except for one of my friends— she tried to warn me that I'd be just one woman among many lining up for Hank."

"Then how'd you know you were special?"

She laughs. "Trust me, it took a while. He had to prove it to me."

"How?" I've heard the story many times before. But not for a long time, and I'll never get sick of it. I could hear it over and over—as many times as Mom is willing to tell me.

"He drew me." She gestures to the drawing on the mantel, the one he made of her when they first met. The one that I'd hoped had a sketch for *Sally in the Stars* on the back but doesn't. He made the drawing while he watched her lecture one day, then gave the drawing to her and told her to keep it, that it might be worth something one day.

"Would you ever sell that drawing?" I ask. "If we needed the money?"

She swallows, like the question is painful for her to answer. "Oh, honey, it's so hard. You know I'd love to keep all of Dad's work forever. Especially the personal ones, like his portrait of me and *G in Blue*. But you never know what'll happen in life. I'll hold on to it all for as long as I can."

Mom tells me how we still have so many things of Dad's to go through, here on our table, and that we can look at more of it together this weekend, because there are some hidden treasures.

"It's all so disorganized and needs to be sorted. And things seem to go missing," she says. "In fact, there's a portfolio of Dad's that I found in one of the boxes I unpacked a couple weeks ago. It's incredible, and I wanted to surprise you with it because it's something very special. For you."

"What is it?" I ask, crossing my fingers that it's not what I think it is.

A smile flickers across her face. "Drawings of you, sweetheart. Like a journal he kept, of your childhood. They're so, so beautiful." She wipes at her eyes.

I freeze. I can't move a muscle, or Mom will suspect. I bite my cheek and squeeze my hands tightly together to keep from saying or doing something I shouldn't.

If the portfolio were still on the table, I could

slip the drawing back in, tonight. Where it belongs.
"Can I see?"

"It's already at the Met. But there's one drawing
that's missing. The last one. I wanted to put it in the
exhibit." She runs her fingers through her hair and
her voice rises in agitation.

"The whole theme is about the intersection of
Dad's personal and artistic lives. So I thought it'd
be great to show some of those drawings of you.
Especially the last one from when you were ten.
Just before he got too sick. I guess I can do without
it. There's a great one from when you were seven.
I could use that." She reaches out and touches my
arm, to soften the blow.

"But I just find it frustrating, and upsetting,
when something like that goes missing. I didn't
have a chance to examine and catalogue it, so
now it's almost like it never existed. I wonder if *I*
misplaced it, somehow, or if someone . . . I don't
even want to consider that. It just *has* to turn up
somewhere."

She sees the expression on my face and asks, "You okay? You haven't seen it, have you?"

I shake my head no, though every cell in my body wants to tell her. That I found it. That I was looking at it in my room and didn't know she needed it and I'll give it right back. But the words won't come. I don't want to disappoint her. She expects more of me—she expects me to handle Dad's art with as much respect as she does. If I tell her what I've done, she'll think I'm just another problem to deal with and that she can't trust me anymore.

For dessert we have brownies with a scoop of vanilla ice cream, but my stomach is so full of worry, I can't bring myself to eat more than a couple bites. I tell her I snuck in a few earlier, so she doesn't question.

After, she goes over to one of the piles of Dad's work and starts sifting through as if she might be able to find the missing drawing, but of course, she won't. "Maybe it fell out of the portfolio, and got mixed up in one of these piles. So many papers . . . Want to help me look now?"

"No, thanks." As I hurry through clearing and washing up the dinner plates, my mind races. I have to get back to my room, to the drawing. I'll take one more look at it, maybe copy it one more time in my own sketchbook, and then put it back on the table. I can slip it into any of these piles, for Mom to "find." So I don't ever have to tell her that I took it.

In my room, I go straight to my desk and pull open the drawer.

But all I see are doodles and mixed-up animal drawings. No *G, age 10.*

It was on top of the pile of papers. I swear it was.

I shuffle through everything, once, then twice, and a third time. Then I empty my drawer—pens, pencils, markers, paper clips, loose staples, pencil shavings, dried-up glue sticks—and go through it all again.

The drawing isn't there.

I think back to the last time I saw it.

Sunday.

With Theo.

CHAPTER

twenty

In a flash I'm out the door, Mom calling after me, "Where are you going?" as I run down the stairs and ring the doorbell of Theo's apartment.

"Coming!" Harriet's voice, and her footsteps approach the door. The pause as she looks through the peephole to make sure it's me. Anyone from outside the building would've had to get buzzed in.

"What a nice surprise, Georgia. Happy Valentine's Day!" Harriet pulls me into a warm hug. It's so good to be in her arms, not to have her question what I'm doing here.

"You, too," I say.

"I could smell some good cooking upstairs. You're treating your mom right today. Lucky Sally."

I nod. I can smell the garlic and chili spices of Thai takeout in their apartment.

"You're here for the boy, aren't you?"

"Yup."

"Go on back."

The door to Theo's room is shut. I barge in to find him at his desk, drawing, as usual. Krypto perches on the desk by Theo's sketchbook, basking in the lamplight.

"Where is it?" I demand, closing his door behind me.

A blast of cold air chills me from his cracked-open window. Theo doesn't seem to notice the layer of snow building up on the windowsill. If I wasn't furious, I'd close the window for him. But no. Let him freeze for all I care.

"What?" Theo looks up, his eyes bleary with concentration.

"The drawing. You took it."

"Me? Um . . ."

It *had* to be him. No one else has been in my room except maybe Mom. And clearly she doesn't have the drawing, or she wouldn't have asked if I'd seen it.

"Theo, where is it?"

"Okay, G, take a deep breath. You're going to kill me—or maybe you won't—but let me explain. Take a seat."

I look down at my usual place on the floor, and for a second, crave that exact right spot, the perfect feeling of comfort—but not today. I stand against the wall, arms crossed. "I'm all ears."

"The other day when I came upstairs, I noticed that drawing you were working on. The one on your desk. And from what I could see, it was something special. I've never seen you draw like that, G. And I just didn't want to let you lose your chance of entering NYC ART. Maybe you haven't been in the mood, but you shouldn't not enter just because . . ."

I'm putting two and two together faster than I'd like as Theo talks. "So you took the drawing and what?"

"I submitted it. To Mr. B. For NYC ART." Theo's voice is a tiny whisper, and his face is like a ghost's. He knows what he did is wrong.

Krypto creeps closer to the edge of the desk. He's about to crawl down. He could run away and get lost in the apartment, or worse—slip through the cracked-open window and out onto the street. But I don't say anything.

"Did you tell Mr. B that you *stole* it from me? That I didn't want to submit anything?"

"Um, no. I kind of pretended that you changed your mind last minute and I was handing it in for you."

"So you stole the drawing and forged an entry sheet from me?"

"Yeah, kind of."

"Oh, Theo, this is bad. Very, very bad."

"I didn't mean for it to be bad! I was trying to

251 ☆

help! It'd be so awesome for us both to get in, to have our first exhibit together. And how could you walk away from the prize money?"

"Easy," I say just as Krypto disappears over the edge of the desk. "I meant it when I said I didn't want to enter. And that was *not* the drawing I would've submitted. In fact, that drawing you *stole* was actually ineligible."

"What? Why?"

"You don't deserve to know." Krypto's halfway across Theo's bedroom floor now, crawling toward the open window. He can crawl right out of Theo's room and into Central Park. Good luck to him.

The last thing I'm going to do now is tell Theo that the drawing is Dad's. Dad's drawing of *me*, with the last asterism sketch. I can't trust him with it. Not anymore. I have to get the drawing back.

I'm about to leave when I take one last look to see Theo at his desk, staring blankly at his sketchbook. He doesn't get it. He doesn't understand why what he did was so bad. I eye the portfolio on Theo's desk where I know he keeps the self-portrait Dad gave him. I want to ask him if I can look at the back for the asterism points I suspect are there. But I don't want to give him the satisfaction that he might have something I want.

Krypto's on the windowsill now, reaching one tentative foot out to the cold air.

"Krypto!" I shout. I can't help it. A vision of him freezing in the snow or being snatched up in the talons of a hawk flashes through my mind. I'd never be able to live with myself.

Theo leaps to his feet and scoops up Krypto in one fell swoop.

I leave before he can even thank me for saving his lizard's life.

The next morning, Friday, I skip-run to school, skirting piles of snow and slush and ice, straight to the art department so I can catch Mr. B before my first class.

"My drawing for NYC ART—I need it." I'm

breathless and my head is spinning and all I can focus on is the drawing. Getting it back.

"What?" He shakes his head, puzzled. "Georgia, it's too late. I delivered the entries on Monday."

My breath catches. "Where is it?"

"At the Met, with the judges. It's quite an experience. I get to hand deliver them to the modern art offices. Have you ever been up there?"

As Mr. B goes on about some of the cool things he saw in the offices, I think how the Met is exactly where Dad's drawing is supposed to be—for Mom's exhibition. But it's in the wrong place.

"I just, I really need my drawing back," I say.

"The only way you could get it back at this point is by withdrawing from the competition. And I was so happy when Theo told me you'd changed your mind last minute and decided to enter. Your entry is fabulous! I bet you have a winner."

If only he knew—that I did not decide to enter, that Theo betrayed me. I wish I could tell Mr. B everything. But the last thing I want is for Mom to find out what I did. And as angry as I am at Theo, I can't tell on him, knowing how devastated he'd be if he got disqualified from NYC ART.

"Then I want to withdraw."

"Withdraw? Seriously? Georgia, I won't let you sabotage yourself."

"But I don't want to win."

Mr. B's face softens. He gives me a long look, like he's trying to see into my mind to figure out why I'm doing this. He probably thinks it's something to do with Dad, my sadness. "Do you really feel that way, Georgia?"

"Yes."

"You're underestimating yourself. That was the best drawing I've ever seen you do."

If only I *had* made that drawing! My chest is tight with a fluttery feeling. I wish I'd faint, get sent to rest in the nurse's office or go home for the day.

The only thing I can do now is to figure out how to get the drawing back—without telling Mom that

I took it or Mr. B that Theo submitted it without my permission.

And the one person who could help me figure out how to do this is the one I'm angriest at right now: Theo. I need him, even if I want to kill him. Because Theo spends his life plotting adventures for Theo-Dare, and for this situation, I could use a bit of help from a superhero.

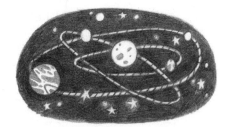

CHAPTER

twenty-one

Theo's and my PE elective is yoga, which means trying to relax our breath on rubber mats stale with sweat. Not the best place to plot out how to solve this muddle we're in.

I place my mat down next to his on the glossy wood gym floor and glare at him. "We need to talk. Meet me at our usual spot after school."

He shrinks back into himself and nods. Good. He should feel awful.

Lying on my back, I close my eyes and try to focus on the teacher's words guiding us to relax our bodies into the floor, to be aware of our breaths, to trace the energy from our heads all the way down into our toes. "Detach your mind," she says, "Start by detaching from your body, then from your thoughts, until you're nothing but breath. Don't think about the next moment and what's to come. You can't control what will happen next, so release yourself from worry."

If only I had no control over what happens next. If only I could stop worrying. But I can't. It's just the opposite: I need to take control, to worry this through, to take action.

Harper walks out of school by herself while I'm waiting for Theo at the gates. All fashionable for the snow, wearing earmuffs and chunky snow boots, she's focused on her phone, her mouth in a flat line. I almost let her walk by me without saying anything. I can't look her in the eye until I know she's returned the money. But then, I'm not much different. What I've done, taking Dad's drawing, is actually far worse. And I remember all the stuff she said, about wanting to be invisible.

I tap her shoulder as she passes.

"Oh, hey." She looks up, her usual cheerful expression plastered back on her face. "What're you up to today? Chloe and Violet have soccer."

"Just going home."

"You still mad at me? About yesterday? I paid the money back, just so you know." She waits for my answer, like she really does care what I think.

"That's okay. I'm not mad." I'm relieved that she paid the money back. And that she thought about it and remembered to tell me. Clearly it weighed on her as much as it did on me. But I also get a twinge of envy for how easily she can fix the thing she did wrong. How easy everything in life seems to be for her.

I imagine living in that enormous house, with parents who own art that costs millions of dollars. Some of their paintings, like the Rothko, are worth enough for thousands of families to live on for their entire lives. And they have it in paint on canvas on the walls of their house. But I also know that even if her life looks perfect from the outside, it doesn't always feel that way for Harper on the inside.

She smiles now, all sunny marigold. "Good. And guess what? We're set for your birthday. My mom got us passes for Wollman Rink. It's going to be so fun!"

As she's describing how she's planned out my whole birthday for Monday, when we have the day off school, with ice-skating, followed by dinner and cake at her house, Theo shows up, shifting the light. His dark copper color casts a shadow on Harper's bright marigold.

Harper gets flustered when she sees him. "Oh, hi! You two hanging out today?"

Depends on what you consider hanging out.

"Can I invite him?" she half whispers to me. I nod.

Theo looks as flustered as Harper does now.

"Me? Ice-skating with you?" Theo squints

behind his glasses as if he thinks we're teasing.

The whole thing makes me burn with embarrassment, but Harper's also acting awkward in a way I haven't seen before.

"Yes, you," she says. "And Chloe and Violet."

"C'mon, Theo, it'll be fun," I say, trying to sound normal.

He puts on his deeper Theo-Dare voice. "Count me in!"

Harper's SUV pulls up just then, putting an end to our awkwardness. "See ya Monday," she calls out the window as the car pulls away.

"That was odd," Theo says on our walk home. "Who'd ever think we'd be celebrating your birthday with those girls?"

"Odder things have happened. Like you stealing my drawing and submitting it to NYC ART." He is so *not* off the hook here.

"Relax, G. It'll be great. You'll be relieved when it wins."

"That's just the point, Theo. It *can't* win."

"*Can't?* Why not?"

"It's not mine."

"What? Then whose . . . ?"

I pause for a second, wishing I didn't have to tell him. But I have no choice. "Dad's."

Theo slaps his hand to his forehead. "Oh, no. Oh. No."

"Oh, yes. Maybe that's why you were so impressed by it."

"You know, it did kind of remind me of your dad's style. Not like I've seen so many of his figurative drawings. But, then how . . ."

I explain it all to him. How I found the portfolio in the piles on our drafting table, and I took that one drawing, to keep it for myself, for a little while.

"Didn't you look at the back?" I ask.

"The back?" He looks chagrined, realizing he should've.

"Yeah, the back of the paper. Where Dad wrote the title of the drawing? *G, age 10*. And also . . ." I hesitate to tell him. But now, for better or worse, Theo is a part of this. And I need to look at his drawing from Dad for proof. "There are pencil points on the back. Like the points of an asterism. Like maybe it was Dad's sketch for the last asterism painting."

"Oh, wow." He's quiet, processing it all, which gives me a few beats to relish the impact of this news on him. Theo gets it—how important that drawing is—and what a big mistake he made. "But how do you know it's really an asterism sketch? Maybe they're just pencil points."

"It's a feeling I have. I can't explain. I saw it, and then it hit me, right away. Instinct, I guess."

"Wow, just, wow. If you're right, G, it could be worth tons of money!"

I roll my eyes. For me, it's not about the money. It's about what it would mean, that I would've been one of Dad's asterisms. "I need to look at the back of the drawing you have. Dad's self-portrait. I bet it has some points on it, too. A sketch for *Man on the Moon.*"

Theo's practically hopping with giddiness,

which makes me regret telling him. This is exactly what I didn't want—to share my discovery and have him think it's his, too.

"But you have to calm down first. Breathe."

"Okay." Theo takes in a deep breath, trying to practice our yoga skills. "So let's think this through. I might own a sketch for an asterism painting. And you might've found a sketch for the last asterism painting. But now it's been submitted to NYC ART. So, what would happen—would it be so bad if the drawing gets into NYC ART? Couldn't you just pretend it's yours?"

"That'd be cheating! The work isn't my own. And it's theft! And on top of all that, Mom knows about the drawing. She's looking for it. She wants to put it in the Met exhibit."

"Oh, boy, this is bad. Okay. Think, think, let's think here. Can you just tell Mr. Butterweit you don't want to enter and you need the drawing back?"

"Tried that this morning. The entries are already in. And you're lucky I didn't tell him what you did. I could get you disqualified."

"But you won't, right? You promise?" He holds out his pinky, and I promise. "Why don't you just tell your mom?"

"Can you imagine what she'd do to me? No way. I have to get it back. Which is why I need you."

Theo begins walking faster, his wheels spinning. "What about the people at the Met? The ones who judge NYC ART?"

My first thought is, *Yeah, right, I'll just barge into the Met and ask them for my entry back.* But then I think about how friendly Evelyn Capstone was, and that maybe I could talk to her. Somehow the thought of asking Evelyn for help is less scary than asking Mom. If she could just give the drawing back to me, no one would have to know what I—or Theo—did.

I tell Theo what I'm thinking, which gets him all pumped up for an adventure. "I know you're majorly pissed at me, but you've gotta admit, this is the perfect story for Theo-Dare and Super G!"

I roll my eyes again. I wish it were a superhero

story, but it's *not*. It's all too real.

Back home, I stop to tell Mrs. Velandry that I need to check something at Theo's before I walk Olive. We go straight to his room. I'm like the secret service, standing guard, watching his every move as he opens his portfolio of extra-special drawings. The very front one is Dad's. He takes it out, handling it like the paper might dissolve into thin air, and holds it up.

Dad. My chest aches. How I wish this were my drawing; I would frame him and put him on my wall and talk to him when I'm in a bad mood or sad or missing him. But it's Theo's. At least he lets me do the honors. He hands me the paper.

I take a deep breath in and hold it, not wanting to let it out until I see. I'll be shattered if there's nothing there.

I turn the paper over.

And there, on the back—pencil points!

I exhale, light-headed and tingly.

I let Theo study the paper and try to keep my trembling thumbs from mistyping as I do a quick search on my phone for *Man on the Moon,* Dad's asterism self-portrait. Holding the image of the painting next to the drawing, it's clear the points on the drawing match up. This is it! A sketch for *Man on the Moon*!

"See." I show Theo.

He looks from the pencil points on the back of the paper to the image of the painting on my phone, and back again. But he doesn't say anything.

I'm frustrated by how quiet he's being. "What? Don't you think I'm right?"

"Yeah, I do. I mean, it's incredible. This is, like, a serious discovery."

"So why don't you sound more excited?"

"Because . . ." He's trying to find the words, and as I study the turmoil in his eyes, I figure it out.

"You're worried my mom's going to take this away from you?" I ask.

He nods.

I know how he feels. Like how I wanted to keep *G, age 10* for myself.

But now, I realize, *G, age 10* isn't a drawing that's meant only for me. Finding the points on the back, the points of me, the proof that Dad planned to paint me for the last asterism, is something the world should know about. I need to get the drawing back, and then somehow explain what I've discovered to Mom.

"Don't worry," I tell Theo. "Dad gave it to you. It's yours, and nothing'll change that. Mom knows that, even if she wants to research it or use it for the exhibit or whatever. It only makes it more special, more important. So just keep it safe for now."

Theo places the drawing carefully back in his portfolio of special drawings.

One thing that's not hard to get is Evelyn Capstone's e-mail address. Mom stays logged in to her e-mail on our home computer, so I just have to open an e-mail from Evelyn and copy the address.

What is hard is deciding what to write. How to ask what I want to ask her. And convincing myself to hit Send even though I know the whole thing could backfire. She could forward the message to Mom, and then Theo and I would be totally busted. But I cross my fingers as I click the Send button.

From: Georgia Rosenbloom
To: Evelyn Capstone
Date: Friday, Feb 15, 4:47 p.m.
Subject: Meeting

Dear Evelyn Capstone,

It was nice to see you last weekend at the Met. I would like to ask you a big favor. Can I come to the office to talk to you? I'm working on a special project for my mother. It's a surprise. So please don't tell her about this message! Thanks!

Yours truly,
Georgia Rosenbloom

From: Evelyn Capstone
To: Georgia Rosenbloom
Date: Friday, Feb 15, 4:55 p.m.
Subject: re: Meeting

Dear Georgia,

I enjoyed seeing you, too, and would be more than pleased to meet with you. A surprise for Sally. How nice! I will keep it between us.

My schedule is quite packed with the upcoming exhibit and judging NYC ART, but how would Thursday, February 21, at 4 p.m. suit you? A day we know your mom won't be at the Met.

Warmly,
Evelyn Capstone

Head Curator, Modern Art
The Metropolitan Museum of Art

My fingers, shaking with nerves, hover over the keyboard. I can't believe it worked, and I'm reassured that Evelyn agreed to keep the meeting between us. Thursday is Mom's teaching day, which means she's usually too busy to check in with me.

But February twenty-first is the day that Theo and I celebrate our birthdays together. The day between our birthdays. He'll have to make up an excuse to Harriet why I'm not home to bake our cake with them. And Mrs. Velandry—I'll have to tell her I can't walk Olive that afternoon.

I don't want to push it by asking Evelyn for another time. She said she's busy, and meeting with me must be a huge favor for her. So I write back: "Yes."

twenty-two

I'm counting down until Thursday when I can meet with Evelyn and get the drawing back. But first there's celebrating my birthday on Monday at Wollman Rink with Theo and the Mermaids.

Theo and I take the bus down Central Park West and walk through the park together. He wants to keep talking about Dad and the asterisms and what I'm going to say in my meeting with Evelyn. But the part of me that wishes I'd kept this all to myself also wants to be alone. For him to stop talking like it's a Theo-Dare adventure and not my real-life problem. For him to know that even though I've made him a part of this, things are far from back to normal.

I tune him out and focus on the snow that still covers the rocks in the park, how it reminds me of a painting by Agnes Martin. A strip of white snow, followed by a strip of gray rock, and above it, the light blue and pink and yellow strips of the sky. I concentrate on those strips of color.

Music blasts through the speakers at the rink, and skaters gather around tables sipping hot chocolate as the Zamboni smooths the ice. We pick up our skate rentals and sit on the benches to put them on. The frayed edges of the laces get caught on the metal hooks.

Harper giggles about how she's never been skating before. She asks Theo to lace her skates for her.

"Ow!" he cries as she accidentally jabs his thigh with her blade, but she just keeps laughing. He looks up at her and smiles. He's feeling the warmth of her sun. I wonder if maybe he's getting a crush back on her. His copper color is shining brighter than ever.

Chloe and Violet can skate. I used to see them at our annual lower school skating party. But now they act helpless and pretend they need Theo to hold them up and help them on to the ice.

So I'm left to myself. The pinch of sharp blades on the rubber matting of the floor on our way over to the rink entrance reminds me of skating with Dad, my first time, in kindergarten. At the skating party. Not all the parents joined in, but Dad did. He held my hand tightly as we looped around and around the ice. And he was the most fun father out there.

Now I step out to join the crowd, feeling like a speck in the universe. Ice-skating in the middle of Central Park, skyscrapers towering overhead, fills me with awe.

Harper skids out of control, and Chloe and Violet's true skating skills shine through as they glide to her aid. We all link arms and do a few loops together, holding up Harper, coaching her. Theo takes off by himself, lapping us.

"This is exhausting." Harper pants, and grabs on to the side wall for a rest.

We stop for a minute and rest with her.

Theo skates toward us, smiling. I want him to end up by my side, like it used to be. But he goes to Harper, who's holding out her hands for him.

"I need your help, Theo," she says.

He links his arms in hers, not even looking at me, and steadies her.

I have the urge to go fast, to make myself dizzy.

"Let's try to spin!" I say to Chloe and Violet.

"Yeah!" Violet says.

The three of us take off toward the center of the ice. We throw ourselves into trying to spin, the edges of our skates carving the ice. We're spiraling away from the center, like planets breaking free of their orbit.

Then it happens. I trip and fall. A strong, definite thud onto my backside.

People around us stop and I hear laughter.

Pain shoots from my bottom up to my neck.

"You okay?" Chloe and Violet come to my side. I try to get up but keep slipping; I can't find my grip on the ice.

"Here." Theo reaches a hand to me. His hands grasp mine and pull me up.

The pain is still there, but it dulls as Theo steadies me.

"Thanks," I say. Theo-Dare, there to save me when I need it. He skates me over to the ramp. I can't get my balance with my pants soaked through to my underwear.

He's about to leave me there, to skate back to Harper and the Mermaids on the other side.

But I hold his hand tight.

It just doesn't feel right, being distant from him. I never really apologized for being mean, and he owes me a real apology for taking Dad's drawing. We're both wrong. I want it to be better. I miss him. Us.

MANY POINTS of Me

"I'm sorry, Theo. Really, truly sorry. I mean it this time. You've always been the best friend to me. And I haven't been the same to you. I'm sorry."

The burning, prickling of tears that I've learned to hold back for the past two years threatens to burst.

And once I let myself, I can't stop. Huge, heaving sobs wrack my body. People around us are looking. For all I know, even the Mermaids are watching.

Theo wraps his arms around me and lets me rest my face on his shoulder, patting my back, shushing in my ear.

We go inside and sit at a table in the corner, with my back to the world. I don't even notice the pain where I fell. It feels like hours before I'm all cried out.

Theo hands me tissues and looks at me like he's never seen me before.

In a way, he hasn't.

It's like I've been hiding since Dad died. I'm not

who I was before. I've been turning into someone else. And Theo and I—we're both just figuring out who that person is.

Who *we* are.

Theo hands me a hot chocolate with whipped cream. It warms my throat down into my belly and calms me.

"I should say sorry, too," he says, cleaning his glasses, which have filled with steam. "And not just for what I did with the drawing. For what I said— about you getting over what happened."

I nod. His apology makes me want to cry even more.

"It's just hard. I never even knew my dad. There're so many nights I can't sleep, wondering who he was. I mean, all I really know is he had red hair." We laugh at that. "And Hank was like a dad to me, too." He holds up his hand to quiet me, as I'm about to interrupt again and tell him how different it is.

I let him continue.

"I know, G, I know he wasn't really my dad, and

that I don't have the same right to him like you do. But at least you knew your dad, and that he loved you. That's the worst thing—my dad didn't love me enough to stick around. Your dad never wanted to leave. He would've given anything to watch you grow up. He would've given up his art for that."

This hits me like a punch in the gut. "How do you know that?"

"He told me. One of the last times I saw him. That's what he said. You're right, G. Life was more important to him than art. And our friendship— that's more important to me than a stupid contest."

At that, the tears start flowing again. Now, we're both crying.

And I realize that Theo hurts, too. It's like I think of Dad's death as something that happened only to me. I don't think about how it affected everyone close to me, too. It wasn't my job at the time—Dr. Markham told me that—to worry about how anyone else was feeling. But now, maybe it's time to start.

Theo and I hug, and we grow stronger, feeling the sadness together.

"There you are. You two lovebirds okay?" Harper's voice brings us back to the present. We pull apart.

She looks hurt, like she thinks she's interrupted a romantic moment between us.

"Yeah, totally fine," I say. "Right, Theo?" We look at each other with a shyness we've never had before.

He smiles back. I don't even care what Harper thinks my relationship is with Theo, because all that matters is that we're getting back to being us. Not us the way we used to be, but a new us.

"Car's picking us up to go back to my house for dinner in fifteen minutes," Harper says, checking her phone. "A few more loops?"

Back out on the ice, I nod at Theo that it's okay if he wants to skate with Harper, that I'm not jealous and they can be friends—or more, if they want—too.

But the last loop, I want for us. "A birthday spin?" I say, gliding up alongside them and grabbing Theo's arm.

And we're off.

I'm glad we go to Harper's house after skating, just so Theo gets a chance to see all the amazing art, too.

"Is this a museum?" he whispers in my ear. "Rothko? Seriously?"

I want to show him Dad's Bird painting *Charcoal on Green* hanging on the landing. But in its place, there's a poster. "The paintings went over to the Met," Mrs. Willis explains.

Harper's parents serve us gourmet burgers and homemade potato chips, followed by a sugar-free, dairy-free, gluten-free carrot cake that her mom bought at a bakery. The green flower decorations on top look professional.

It's no pizza and homemade cake full of butter and sugar, which is what Theo and I always have.

"We'll still do our usual, right?" I say to him when we have a quiet moment away from the Mermaids.

He nods.

A Harper-hosted birthday is fun, but it doesn't seem like the party is really for me. More for her, which makes me feel empty inside, not filled.

And when I get home and Dad's paintings, G in Blue, Glimpse of Light, and Figure in the Dark, are gone again—which I should've realized, after seeing the Willises' painting was down—I feel even emptier.

Wednesday is my actual birthday. February twentieth. I'm twelve years old, but I don't feel any different than I did the day before. Except that I'm one year further away from losing Dad.

Mom has an oversized chocolate cupcake with rainbow confetti sprinkles for me, topped with a one candle and a two candle, for dessert that night. But we're saving the real celebration for the next day, February twenty-first, with Theo and Harriet. Like always.

Except this year, I'm not going to be able to help make the cake. My meeting with Evelyn at the Met is more important than any birthday celebration. If I accomplish my mission of getting G, *age 10* home, safe and sound, without having to tell Mom about the whole thing—that would be the best birthday present ever.

CHAPTER

twenty-three

Theo and I do our usual walk home together after school on Thursday, but nothing is as usual, because we have a Theo-Dare–designed plan to get my drawing back.

Theo'll tell his mom that I promised Mrs. Velandry that I'd walk Olive, and that I don't mind taking a break from the baking this year. And I'll tell Mrs. Velandry that I can't walk Olive, because I'm baking a cake. It's not like Mrs. Velandry or Harriet will check in with each other and catch me out. Then, at the Met, I'll have to convince Evelyn to give me back my entry.

Entry in hand, I'll go straight home and slip the drawing into a pile on the table before Mom gets back from work. We'll have our birthday dinner and cake. And some time in the next few days, I'll offer to help Mom look through the piles, and we can "find" the drawing. Simple as that.

"I can't lie to Mrs. Velandry's face," I tell Theo when we turn onto our block. "Can I just write a note instead?"

"Hmm, that's not a bad idea, actually. Avoids the risk of you breaking down and telling her everything."

But when we approach our building, Mrs. Velandry is watching for us, as always. She holds Olive in her arms like a baby and waves Olive's front paw hello at me. I feel guilty disappointing them.

"That's okay," Mrs. Velandry says when I tell her I can't walk Olive because it's Theo's and my birthday celebration (which isn't exactly a lie).

"Will you come up and celebrate with us tonight?" I ask her.

"I'll try," she says. "But you know how I am about going out!"

"It's hardly *going out*," Theo scoffs from where he's waiting for me on the building stairs, after Mrs. Velandry has relocked her door.

Hardly *going out* compared to what I'm about do. "Wait—I can't just go back out the main door now. Mrs. Velandry will see me leave."

Theo thinks quick. "The basement," he says. "Use the building service entrance."

Ugh. I do *not* like going down to our basement, where the laundry room is, alone, and if I've ever gone out the service entrance, it's with Theo.

"Here, I'll go with you," he offers, sensing my hesitation.

We walk down the stairs to the basement, crossing fingers that no one will be doing laundry, that there won't be any mice or cockroaches. The basement, empty and dark, smells of damp and detergent. Theo switches on his phone's flashlight to guide us through the winding hallways. We get to the square window of natural light on the service door and walk up the steps that lead to it. Theo pushes through and holds the door open for me.

A blast of fresh air hits me as I step out onto the street, around the corner from the main entrance of our building. Out of Mrs. Velandry's sight. "I wish you'd come with me!" I can't help but say.

I know Theo wishes he could, too. "That would be too suspicious. But here, take this." He takes his lucky eraser, the paint palette–shaped one, out of his pocket and presses it into my hand. It's reassuring when I wrap my fingers around it.

"Wish me luck." We do our double fist-bump handshake.

I can't waste time and wait for the bus—it's 3:40 p.m. and my 4 p.m. meeting is fast approaching—so I hail a taxi, using my allowance to pay for it to take me across town to the Met.

When I get out of the taxi on Fifth Avenue, my

instinct is to hunch and bend my head against the frigid wind, but I throw my shoulders back and lift my chin. I'm not a scared child going to meet with her mom's boss; I have business to do, and I'm going to accomplish my goal. I have to. The other choice is telling Mom what I did with Dad's drawing. And risk getting Theo disqualified from NYC ART.

I pull open the glass doors to the side entrance and march up to the security desk with confidence.

The guard asks me who I'm here to see. I give him Evelyn's name and my name. I wait nervously while he calls up to her, looking around the walls of the education center, where the winning entries of NYC ART will be on display when the exhibit opens in April. Where I used to imagine my own entry hanging one day.

A young woman in an ankle-length skirt, cardigan, and heels, walks toward me with a welcoming expression on her face. "I'm Jenna, Evelyn's assistant. You must be Georgia Rosenbloom." She extends her hand toward me. "So nice to meet you. I thought it was so cool when Evelyn told me you're Hank and Sally's daughter. I never knew your dad, but I love his work, and your mom is just the best."

I smile at her, wishing I had something clever to say, but I'm just hoping she won't say anything about me to my mom next time she sees her.

"Sorry," she says. "I'm talking your ear off! And I know this is about a surprise for your mom— Evelyn's waiting in her office."

As we pass the familiar route up the stairs to the first floor, through the Greek and Roman galleries, the African galleries, and into the modern galleries, Jenna chatters away about how she's new on the curatorial staff and lucky to have the opportunity to work on the show.

We take the stairs to the second floor, to the gallery with a Chuck Close and an Andy Warhol painting.

We reach the empty spot where *Sally in the Stars*, Dad's asterism painting of Mom, usually hangs.

But now, across from that wall, there's a barrier in front of the smaller series of side galleries where Dad's exhibition is going to open in a couple of months. A framed poster with the image *Sally in the Stars* advertises it. In dark gray, bold letters, it reads: *Hank Rosenbloom: Artist and Man.*

"It's going to be amazing, isn't it?" Jenna says. "Studying your father's art is what made me decide I wanted to pursue art history."

The full meaning of it all hits me. How thousands of people—strangers—will come to the Met, to these galleries, to look at Dad's paintings. How the three asterism paintings are going to hang together for the first time. How there's still a big question mark, a blank canvas, where the last asterism painting should be.

A question I can answer. A blankness I can fill. With the pencil points on the back of *G, age 10.*

I follow Jenna into the modern art department and down the corridor to Evelyn's office. I'm struck, right away, by seeing the three asterism paintings together again. *Sally in the Stars,* reunited with *Bird in the Tree* and *Man on the Moon.* I haven't seen them all together like this since they left Dad's studio one at a time. The three equal-sized canvases tower over me, forming a giant window in the wall of Evelyn's office. I half expect Dad himself to appear, pull me into a side hug, and say, "Let's take a closer look together, sweetheart. Tell me what you see in these paintings. How do they make you feel?"

But there's only Evelyn Capstone, like the queen of Dad's art, sitting on her throne above her loyal subjects. She's sitting behind her sleek wooden desk, with her back to the window, illuminated by the midday light.

I feel for Theo's lucky eraser in my pocket and give it a squeeze.

"Here she is. Georgia Rosenbloom!" Jenna announces me.

"Thank you, Jenna." Evelyn nods her head in dismissal, and Jenna leaves us alone.

"Have a seat." Evelyn gestures to the two wooden chairs across from her desk.

I sit in the one closer to Dad's paintings. The chair is stiff as a board. It keeps me upright and makes me straighten my posture.

"Isn't it wonderful, seeing Hank's asterisms here, together like this?"

I nod.

"It's a bit unconventional to keep them in the curator's office. The other paintings are in conservation, but I just couldn't help myself with the asterisms. I wanted to be surrounded by them for inspiration as I work on my catalogue essay." She smiles. "The Q&A your mother did with that boy, Theo Goodwin, is just darling. Shame you didn't want to participate."

Oh, little does she know.

"Now." Evelyn clasps her hands under her chin. "Tell me about this special surprise project you're working on for your mother?"

twenty-four

I squint at Evelyn Capstone, trying to see her form solidly against the glare of the window, to figure out what color I'd use for her. Fuchsia, like the color of the blouse I saw her in last time.

"Um, there isn't really a project. I just needed a reason—actually—it's about NYC ART."

I expect for her to be angry that I lied, but she looks amused instead. "I see. What about NYC ART?"

"I'm—I was—I want to get my entry back."

She cranes her neck forward even more than

usual and gives me a questioning look. "Did you enter? When I saw you last, you seemed quite sure that you weren't going to."

Ah, of course. Having to lie now and tell her that I decided to enter makes me want to be sick. But I have to do it.

"I entered at the last minute," I say, surprised at how easy it is. "But it was the wrong decision. So I came to see you, to get it back."

"Why would you want to do that?"

I wish I could tell her why. The truth. But you have to save your truths for the people who won't judge you. The ones who hear the bad thing you did and love you anyway, like Theo. Evelyn Capstone is not that person for me.

But I can tell her something. Not the whole truth—a part of it.

"Because—it's not mine." The same words I used to explain to Theo last week. I think fast how to answer what I know will be her next question.

"This is an interesting situation." She leans

back in her chair and looks at me almost with a new respect, as if she didn't think I was capable of acting so out of line. "Then whose, may I ask, is it?"

"I can't tell you," I say, fully resolved. "For now—all I can tell you is that I've done something wrong. And a friend is also involved. I mean, nothing illegal—nothing dangerous—" Evelyn's hand goes to her phone as if she might be about to call Mom, or security or something. "It's personal, and it's wrong, and I know I have to fix it. I just need to get the drawing back, and then tell my mom. And then I promise, I'll fix everything."

Evelyn takes her hand off the phone, and raises an eyebrow. "Truly an unexpected situation. I don't know what to make of it, but I respect the guts it takes to have gotten yourself here and told me this much, at least. So as long as you promise me that you're going to tell your mother first thing, and you're going to fix this situation—whatever it is— I'll agree to give you the entry back. And you know I'll be seeing her to make sure, tomorrow."

As she speaks, and as the clouds roll in, shading the brightness of the sun, her color becomes clearer, brighter.

"Thanks," I say, feeling shy around her, as always, but a little less so. "I promise."

"Before we find your entry, I want to remind you what I said to you the other day: getting into NYC ART isn't everything. In the end, it's just a contest, and there's always a certain amount of randomness in the outcome. Not everyone gets in, but that doesn't mean those who don't, won't go on to become successful artists. And maybe you'll find you don't want to be an artist, after all. You don't have to follow in your father's footsteps." She looks me in the eyes. "So what I'm trying to say, Georgia, is you be you. Got it?"

"Got it."

"Good." She sits back and smiles. "Mini-lecture over—relax!"

I let out a giggle. I feel like I've unwrapped a scarf that's too hot and itchy from around my neck, making me able to breathe again.

"So there's no special project for your mom?" she asks.

"No," I say. But in a weird way, I realize, this *is* for Mom—for both of us. Proving Dad's last asterism. "Actually, sort of. Yes."

"Well, I can't wait to see what it is." Evelyn shakes her head and sighs. "Come on. Let's go to the conference room to find your entry."

We get to the door of a windowless room, with metal shelves that are filled with files and boxes and a long conference table covered with paintings, drawings, sculptures, collages, photographs— NYC ART entries.

I look at the entries spread out on the table. These must be entries by older students. They look professional. There's an oil on canvas of a girl in shades of blues and greens that's so powerful, I know it has to be a top contender. A clay sculpture of a boy's head that looks like it could rival an ancient Roman portrait bust. But I don't see my entry—Dad's drawing—or Theo's, either.

Evelyn and Jenna look up my entry number and its location on the computer.

They pull up my entry, and Evelyn shows me how they're striking a big red line through it with the word *withdrawn.*

Then Jenna goes to one of the file drawers along the wall and comes back with a manila folder.

As soon as the folder's in my hands, I flip it open for a quick glance to make sure the drawing is safe and sound inside. It's like I've been missing the last piece of a thousand-piece jigsaw puzzle, and I've finally found it, and everything can go back to fitting together just right.

Dad's drawing is back with me, where it's meant to be. Now I have to return it to its rightful place, with Mom.

"Will you show us?" Evelyn asks as I go to slide it in my backpack.

"Um, not now." As much as I want to show it to her and tell her everything I've discovered, I'm proud of myself for staying strong. Mom deserves to know first. "But I think you'll get to see it soon."

In the Hank Rosenbloom exhibition.

Outside the world is surreal. Different.

I feel different. Changed.

I walk home through Central Park to let my heart rate slow back to normal.

A flicker of red on one of the branches catches my eye in the dusky light. A cardinal. The background is not pure snowy white, like in Dad's bird painting, *Red on White*. But still. It's beautiful. And it's looking at me.

Dad's the one who told me about cardinals. He taught me to listen for their song. He said that some people believe that when a cardinal comes, it's a dead person visiting you.

"Maybe it's Grandpa," I'd said.

Dad had just smiled. He was sick then. Maybe he already knew that he was going to die. And he was telling me to look for him after.

The cardinal chirps its song above me, *Dooh-dooh duh dooh-dooh.*

I imagine it's Dad. Here to tell me he's watching and still with me. A few weeks ago, the thought of Dad being here and watching me would've comforted me. But I'm not so sure I'd want Dad to see me now. To know what I've done. Even if I convinced myself that Dad somehow meant the drawing for me, it wasn't mine to take. I could've lost it for good.

I look at the cardinal to see if he's disappointed in me, like I am in myself. But he's not even really looking at me. I'm just imagining that.

The cardinal is not Dad.

Dad is gone.

The cardinal is just a beautiful red bird.

And I'm all alone.

But I'm ready for it.

Ready to figure out my own way.

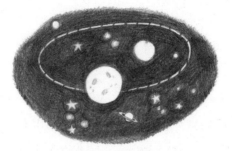

CHAPTER
twenty-five

I sense the drama ahead as soon as I enter our building. Mrs. Velandry's door is open and she's pacing the lobby with Olive in her arms. My heart drops.

"Oh, Georgia, there you are! Your mom called because Harriet told her that she missed you for cake baking, so she wanted to know if you were back from walking Olive, and I told her that you never walked Olive because you were with Theo, and now everyone's in a panic! Check your phone. Your mom's been trying to reach you."

I pull my phone from my backpack, and sure enough, while I had the ringer off in the museum, there were five missed calls from Mom. There're also texts from Theo, warning me.

"I'm okay—everything's fine," I say. "I don't want them all to worry. Can we just tell them I fell asleep?"

Mrs. Velandry shakes her head sadly, like she too wishes she could go back in time. "I used the spare key to go in to your apartment to check for you, and I told her you weren't there. I didn't even see you leave. How did you get out?"

"Um, I walked." Of course, that's not the answer she's looking for

I run through possible lies in my head: I wanted to be alone today, so I went to get something to eat, to the library, for a walk to get fresh air. So many lies.

But I'm ready to tell Mom everything—not that I even have a choice, anymore. I promised Evelyn. I just need to prepare myself. "Where's Mom now?"

"She's on her way home. Come, sit with me. Have something to eat while you're waiting."

My stomach is in such knots at what I'm going to say to Mom, what she'll say to me, that I don't think I can eat. But the smell of zucchini bread wafts out of Mrs. Velandry's apartment.

Olive leaps from Mrs. Velandry's arms as she puts her down inside the apartment. I take a seat at the table. She cuts a large chunk of steaming fresh bread for me and sets it on the table.

Usually Olive would beg for food at my feet. But today she sticks to her bed, hardly paying me attention.

"She's still sad about Royal," Mrs. Velandry says. "The missing never goes away, does it? It just becomes a part of who you are."

I nod, taking a bite and letting the bread fill my insides.

Mrs. Velandry goes over to her messy desk and rummages through some papers. "I found those drawings I was telling you about. Your dad's sketches for the bird paintings. Ah, here they are."

She sets a stack of loose papers down on the table before me.

The first drawing shows the regal lines of a blue jay. I feel the same tingle as when I first found the portfolio with the drawings of me. I know I was there when Dad got the inspiration and when he made these drawings. In this very room, at this very table. His art is a part of me; I am a part of his art. That's how Dad lives on.

"They're special, aren't they?" Mrs. Velandry says.

"Yes." But I don't explain what makes them even more special to me.

"You can have them."

"Really? But he gave them to you. They might be worth something. See, he even signed them."

"I always meant to give them to you. When you were old enough to be responsible. How old are you now, anyway? Eleven?"

"I turned twelve yesterday."

"Yes, of course. Happy birthday. They're yours. Take them." She stacks the papers together and hands them to me, like they're sections of the newspaper.

I go through the pile on my lap, turning each page

over and looking even more carefully at the backs.

And, almost three-quarters through, on the back of the sketch for the cardinal in the snow, *Red on White*, are pencil points! Ones that I just know will match up to the asterism painting *Bird in the Tree*.

My heart flutters. I now have sketches for three asterism paintings.

And then the building door clangs open. Frantic footsteps follow, and a knock at Mrs. Velandry's door.

Mom.

"Mrs. Velandry?" she calls.

Mrs. Velandry unlocks the door and Mom bursts through, panicked in a way I haven't seen her in years. It's like she's forgotten to worry about *me* all this time, and she's suddenly remembered that I might not always be safe, either.

"Georgia! Where were you? Are you okay?"

"I'm fine, Mom. Everything's okay. I just—"

"Then I don't know what explanation there could possibly be!" Mom's voice is shrill, and the worry on her face turns to anger. "You told Harriet you were walking Olive, and Mrs. Velandry that you were baking a cake? And then, you—you just prance back in here like it doesn't even matter!"

"Sally, she's here. She's okay." Mrs. Velandry touches Mom's shoulder. "Sometimes we make mistakes."

Mom nods, her eyes glistening.

"I'm sorry, Mom," I whisper, clutching the bird drawings that Mrs. Velandry gave me against my chest. They make me feel safe.

Mom notices the papers now. "And what are these?"

"Dad's drawings." I hold them out to show her.

"You mean the one that's missing?" she asks, confused. "The portrait of you?"

"No, not that. Birds."

Mrs. Velandry and Olive swivel their heads between Mom and me.

"It sounds like you two have some talking to do." Mrs. Velandry hands me my backpack and walks us to the door.

"Yes," Mom says. "We do."

CHAPTER

twenty-six

"Mom," I say, as soon as we're inside the tiny elevator. "I have the drawing that you're looking for, too."

"What do you mean?"

For a split second, the elevator jolts as if it's going to get stuck, but it keeps going up. And everything comes out in a rush, my heart pounding a rhythm beneath my confession.

I tell Mom how I looked through Dad's portfolio and decided to keep the one drawing, *G, age 10*, for myself. I was so jealous of Theo and what he had that I didn't, and I thought if I could just have one thing for myself, that's all that mattered. But then Theo submitted the drawing, and I wanted to get it back without having to tell her what we'd done.

Mom shakes her head. I want her to say something, anything, even to yell at me and tell me how angry she is and what I did was wrong.

But for once, Mom is speechless. Instead, she wraps her arms around me, and pulls me close. "I should be so, so angry at you right now," she whispers. "And I am. But I'm also . . . I don't know yet. Let's see this drawing."

We go into our apartment and sit down at the drafting table, which has some open space. There aren't as many piles as before. The exhibition is getting closer.

I take the folder out of my backpack and pull out the drawing. There's G, *age 10* on the table.

It's quiet except for me and Mom, breathing softly. And another presence, too. Dad, reaching us, through the marks on the page.

"There she is." Mom traces the lines of the drawing, lightly, lovingly. Like I did when I first saw it, and for the days after every time I looked at it. "She's beautiful."

She means me. At age ten. The way Dad drew me, then. Beautiful.

I bite the sore on the inside of my cheek, which isn't actually so sore anymore. It's healed a bit the last couple of weeks. But I bite it as I flip the drawing over to show Mom the back. The part she maybe doesn't know about.

"Mom, I think I know what this is."

Her reaction tells me it's true.

"Is this a sketch—for the last asterism?" She puts her hand to her mouth. "Georgie, this is everything."

Mom squeezes me, hugging me tight. We're both sobbing, so you can't tell where she ends and I begin. They're not just tears of sadness, though. It's not just about losing Dad. It's also about finding something new: the joy and relief of this discovery.

We sit like that, together, until the tears slow.

"And there's more, Mom. Look." I set the bird drawing before her. The one of the cardinal in the snow, that I just got from Mrs. Velandry. "Turn it over."

"Oh, wow." Mom's eyes gleam. She presses one palm to her chest and touches her other to the paper. "Can you believe that Mrs. Velandry's had it all these years?"

Her lips twitch and spread into a smile. "And I might have one, too!" She goes to her room and comes back with a portfolio. Like the one I found the drawings of me in. One of Dad's.

She flips it open. It's empty except for one drawing, which she slides out of the plastic sleeve. A drawing of her. Like the one on our mantel, but this one looks less finished. And on the back: the points. A sketch for the asterism of *Sally in the Stars*.

Mom sets it down next to the other two, the bird and *G, age 10.*

"I checked the other drawing." I point to the frame on the mantel. "But it wasn't that one."

"Good thinking," Mom says. "You wouldn't have known to look for this one. I've always kept it private, just for me. Dad made it soon after we got married. I never thought much about the pencil points before. I always assumed he was using the points to guide his lines. Or they were just random doodles. But now it's so obvious. I know—*we* know."

I feel a glow inside, that I'm the one who brought it to her attention.

"Georgie, do you understand what an incredible discovery this is? We can use these in the exhibit. It's going to make it all come together, to show these first sketches of Dad's process in making the asterism paintings."

"I know where the last one is, too." I'm hesitant to tell her about Theo's drawing, the sketch for *Man on the Moon*, because I know he won't want to give it up, even if just for the exhibit. But he'll have to. It's too important for him—for anyone—to keep private anymore.

"Theo?" she asks.

I nod. Of course, Theo.

I get that twinge of jealousy again. The irritation like dirt in my eye, that Theo's a part of this, even though Dad wasn't truly *his* father. But then, Dad didn't paint him—he wasn't going to be the last asterism. It was me. And more than that—there was enough of Dad to go around for all of us: for me, Mom, Theo, even Royal and Mrs. Velandry. And for the whole world—everyone who loves his art, all the people who will come to the exhibit to see his paintings. That's why we speak of artists in the present tense, that's how Dad still *is*.

"Mom—does this change your Q&A with Theo for the catalogue? I mean, Dad must've thought of painting asterisms before that night when Theo asked him if he'd tried to paint the stars. If this drawing is from when you got married, and he made the bird drawing when I was a toddler . . . that was way before that night."

Mom sits back in her chair to consider the

question. "He told Theo that he hadn't yet painted the stars, but that doesn't mean the idea hadn't already occurred to him. It seems clear from the sketches here that he'd doodled ideas for asterisms for a long time. But he didn't go full force ahead with it—actually making the paintings—until Theo's question. So, Theo's anecdote is still important. Sometimes it takes a direct question like Theo's to make an artist's idea come together. But it also takes someone like you noticing things like the points on the back of the drawing to bring these discoveries to light."

That twinge of jealousy I feel for Theo seeps out of me as Mom talks. Because as we sit quietly together, looking at the three asterism sketches lined up on the table, I think about how Dad used to call me and Theo his binary stars. Now I realize there's enough light for both our stars to shine.

Despite everything that's happened, we still celebrate. More than just our birthdays this time.

Theo and Harriet come upstairs, Theo with a bunch of foil balloons in our favorite colors—green-blue stars for me and red hearts for him. Krypto perches on his shoulder. Harriet holds the round cake with M&M's on top that form the number twelve.

Mom wipes at her eyes. "Looks delicious!" she says. "Happy birthday, Theo!"

"And happy birthday to you, dear Georgia," Harriet says. "You all okay?" She puts the cake down on the table and goes to Mom's side. Mom, who's nodding and still wiping at tears in her eyes, but smiling at the same time.

"It's always an emotional time of year, isn't it?" Harriet says, pulling Mom into a hug. Because of Dad. The time of year he was sick, two years ago.

"And, there's this." Mom gestures to the drawings on the table. Harriet and Theo come up to take a closer look. Even Krypto seems to be curious.

Harriet doesn't get it—all she sees are pencil points on the back of paper.

But Theo gets it, right away. His eyes twitch,

his jaw drops open. "Are these . . . ?"

I nod, the grin on my face spreading wider.

"You got it back?" he whispers. I'll fill him in later, but for now, I just hand him back his lucky eraser.

Mom explains to Harriet that these are initial sketches for Dad's asterism series. Simple little jots, which maybe didn't mean a lot to him, but mean everything to us. Especially the sketch for the last asterism, G, *age 10*.

And I say, "Theo, your turn."

"Now?" he asks, making sure it's okay, that Mom knows everything. I nod.

"I'll be right back." He hands me Krypto to hold while he runs back to his apartment and returns a minute later with his drawing—the self-portrait of Dad.

He places it facedown on the table. On the back, the pencil points of the asterism for *Man on the Moon*. It completes the series of four asterism sketches. Together, we make things whole.

☆ ☆ ☆

Twelve turns out to be the most mixed-up birthday celebration ever. Eleven was my first without Dad. It was a blur; I barely even remember.

Twelve—with a piece of chocolate cake, a scattering of M&M's, the asterism sketches, and even Mrs. Velandry—feels like everything that got mixed up when Dad died is getting sorted out. All the different parts of me have been put back together in a new way.

That night there's a super moon. The full moon is closest to the Earth in its orbit. We can see it through our living room windows—glowing huge and bright. Like the moon is checking in on us, coming to give us a birthday hug.

"Let's go outside to see it better!" Theo suggests.

"Great idea!" Mom says, even though it's freezing cold. "Oh, but I couldn't find the key."

Mrs. Velandry gives me a look.

"Um, I have it," I whisper. Mom's confused, but

she just shakes her head, doesn't bother to ask me how or why.

We step out onto the balcony, to get a better look at the moon. The balcony that isn't the same without Dad. But a place where I can imagine him with us. Or if not with us, up there, in that large round disc of a moon. Watching us.

The moon's orbit around the earth is not a perfect circle. Tidal and gravitational forces pull on the moon, affecting its orbit. Just like my orbit, and Theo's orbit, are not perfect circles, either. We don't always follow the same path. But we always come back together at some point.

"I heard on NPR today that the super moon appearing larger to us is an illusion," Harriet says. "They call it the 'moon illusion.' The moon seems huge when it's rising on the horizon in comparison to objects next to it. But it's not actually that much bigger."

I try to ignore her comment, which takes away the magic of what we see with our eyes, and bask in the glow of the moon. I imagine Dad up there, making his mark in the lunar dust. Maybe one day I'll meet him up there and make my mark next to his.

But for now, I need to make my mark down here on Earth.

When Theo and I blow out the candles, we each make a private wish. I don't know what he wishes for. Maybe to get in to NYC ART, maybe that Harper can be his girlfriend. Or that one day, he'll find his father.

I wish that from today on, the new me will start to feel less mixed up. I'm becoming less like a cut-paper silhouette and more like a Louise Nevelson sculpture—lots of different pieces that don't seem to fit together, but make sense as a whole once they're placed in the same work of art.

I apologize to Theo again, for everything. Even for cutting the piece of Dad's toe out of the photograph. I give it back to him, in case he wants to tape it back together.

The Dad-piece that's missing in me won't ever get filled or replaced. But other parts will shift over it, and it won't feel like such an empty space anymore. It'll begin to feel like it's somehow, impossibly, okay to be that way.

twenty-seven

Mom and Harriet want us to tell Mr. Butterweit what happened first thing on Friday. But I beg off because of being exhausted and overwhelmed and ask to wait until Monday, which they agree to.

Also, I have something I haven't had in the longest time: inspiration. I want to have a real self-portrait ready to turn in when we talk to him.

I decide to go to the planetarium at the Museum of Natural History that weekend, because it will put me in the right frame of mind. I invite Harper and Theo to come with me.

Going to the space show reminds me of Dad. When I was little and couldn't fall asleep, Dad would take me on what he called "nighttime walks." The world outside felt different, in my pajamas, when the sky was dark and children were supposed to be sleeping.

We'd look at the stars from the park. But you can't see them very well there, with all the bright lights of the city. Dad promised to take me camping upstate one summer so we could see the stars for real. That won't happen now, not with him, but at least I still have the planetarium. And I know I'll do that camping trip, someday.

Theo, Harper, and I settle into large, comfy seats below the screen arced overhead like a sky. The lights dim. Sitting in the middle, between my friends, I get lost in the darkness.

We learn that the stars continuously crush inward, and gravitational friction causes their interiors to heat up. The energy in their centers makes them appear to shine.

We also learn about the far side of the moon—how one side of the moon always faces away from Earth. Its terrain is rugged with craters, and no human being has ever set foot there. You only ever get to see half the moon. You never get to see the whole thing.

The moon is as familiar as anything in our lives. But a part of it is always hidden, out of sight. Just like with people: we have all these different sides of us, and sometimes you only know one side of a person. Or you discover another side that you never knew was there before.

Like I have the lighter side of me, the Harper side. But I can still have the deeper Theo side, too.

That's when it comes together, like I hoped it would. Like Theo's question made the idea come together for Dad. *My* self-portrait idea, my Truth. A way to complete the ten pencil points Dad made on the back of *G, age 10*. The last asterism—in my own vision.

As we walk down the exit ramp from the space

show, Harper's bubbling with plans, other parts of the museum she wants to explore.

"Dinosaurs are awesome," Theo says. "I used to go every weekend."

"Let's go now!" Harper says.

But I just want to get home to my art supplies. "You two enjoy."

At home, the first thing I do is march up to the wooden trestle where Dad's paint cans are stored. No one's touched them in nearly two years. The metal is cool, and dusty. I take down one of the black paints and try to open the lid. Of course, it's stuck. So I use the metal edge of a screwdriver to pry it open.

That smell. The mix of car fumes and grass. It smells right.

The paint has separated, with a thin congealed skin on top. I remove it, and use a stir stick to blend the paint and liquid back together. They're not too dried up, after all. A few good stirs does the trick. I open a few more cans of black paint and do the same.

Then I take the fourth wood panel, the one I didn't even bother trying to make for my lunar dust portrait. I paint the background black, mixing the different pigments in a way that feels good. It flows; doesn't feel forced. The vision is there in my head, and my hand is capturing it the way I see it. Everything is working together.

When it's finished, I let it dry. And then I take a piece of tracing paper and use a thick pencil to draw myself. Not how Dad drew me at age ten, but how I am now, nearly two years later, at age twelve. I don't even look in the mirror to do it. I don't think too much. I just let the pencil move, trusting it will come out right. And it does. I trace over the pencil lines with my silver paint pen.

I mark twelve asterism points on the drawing of me. And I mix tempera to paint each point of me in a different color. Ones that represent everyone in my life: copper, aqua, marigold, fuchsia, green, mauve, burgundy, beige, olive, neon orange, royal blue. Colors that are kind of random, that you wouldn't think fit together well, but somehow, on the dark outer space background, they do.

I pause to figure out a color that represents me. But, still, all I see is gray. Only it's less charcoal now and more silver. It has a sparkle to it after all.

The paint is still wet enough for me to lay the tracing paper on top. I use a thin layer of glaze to set the tracing paper onto the black background. And let the whole thing dry.

Mom peeks in to tell me to go to sleep as it's getting late. I try to hide my painting, but she catches a glimpse, and I see the pride on her face.

When I finish, in the early hours of the morning, I know it's good. Powerful. They're *my* asterism points. Not Dad's. And I feel his approval somewhere deep inside of me.

I have the perfect title for it, too. *Georgia in Orbit.* I don't know if that's what Dad would've called it, if he'd had the chance to make the last asterism. But it's the right one for me.

As I try to fall asleep, I think about how time is

supposed to be steady and constant, but it doesn't always go that way. Sometimes time feels slow and takes forever.

And sometimes it feels like it's moving at the speed of light, and I can't stop.

In science class Dr. Anders says that the speed of light in a vacuum is actually a constant. It travels 186,000 miles per second.

Maybe if I could travel at the speed of light, I could hurtle off this planet into orbit and float peacefully among the stars, too far away to care about all the little things happening on Earth.

But here I am, firmly weighted down by gravity. Hurtling toward Monday. Time for Theo and me to tell Mr. Butterweit everything.

On Monday morning, clouds threaten rain on our walk to school. Theo and I find Mr. B in the art studio before first period, sketching at his desk.

"Hi," I say.

"Oh, hi." He looks up, and shuts his sketchbook,

like he doesn't want us to see his work. "Nice surprise to see you two. What's up?"

I know what's on our minds, but I wonder what's on his. We're always sharing our work with him, but he keeps his drawings private. "Can we see what you're working on?" I ask, stalling for time.

"Well, okay, but only for you. I get a little insecure about my work, just like anybody else."

He flips open the sketchbook to the most glorious landscapes. Fantastical, magical landscapes, with princesses and knights, dragons and unicorns.

"Cool! I love these." He lets us flip through a few pages.

"They look like illustrations," Theo says.

"They are. For a picture book I'm working on. My wife wrote the story, and I'm doing the illustrations."

"Can we read it?" Theo asks.

"Someday, I hope." He smiles. "Now, what about you?"

There's only one way to begin, and I'm the one

who has to do the talking, as Theo's mouth clamps shut. "We need to talk to you about NYC ART."

Mr. B gives me a worried look. "Is this about wanting to withdraw your entry?"

Having Theo here, by my side, gives me the strength I need to tell Mr. Butterweit the whole story. I warm up to it, and Theo relaxes a little, even adding a few comments here and there, but he's more nervous than I am. In a way, he has more to lose.

When we finish, Mr. B's confused look turns to sympathy. "Oh, my. This is a first." He leans back in his chair and puts his hand to his forehead, like he's trying to work out a problem. "I'm not even sure who to reprimand here, if anyone. It sounds like you both did something wrong in this situation, and tried to fix it on your own, and everything's worked out, but I'll still need to discuss it with your mothers and come up with some sort of consequence for these actions."

Theo and I nod. I have something else to share with them.

"I ended up making a real self-portrait." I reach into my backpack for the panel that I brought with me. My asterism self-portrait.

"I'm calling it *Georgia in Orbit*," I announce proudly, setting it out on Mr. B's desk for them to admire.

We all look at it together. Under the fluorescent lights of the art studio, the black glows brighter than at home, and the multicolored points of the asterism seem to twinkle, like real stars.

Theo gives my arm a squeeze.

In the silence of us looking, I notice another sound. The steady rhythm of rain on the windows. The skies have let loose. It makes it even cozier, safer inside the studio.

"You nailed it here." Mr. B nods. "This one, this is awesome. It's too late for NYC ART, but that doesn't matter. It's only a competition. Still, I'm disappointed that I used one of our entries on you, Georgia, when there might've been other deserving artists in our class. And, Theo, this could be grounds for me to notify the judges and disqualify you—"

He sees the horrified looks on our faces, and he softens. "But I won't. I think you've learned enough of a lesson on your own."

I nod, grateful that Theo won't lose his chance to get in to NYC ART, but I wonder what lesson, if any, I've learned. That art competitions don't matter all that much? That you risk losing everything when you take a drawing that doesn't belong to you? Or that it's worth the risk, when you end up proving that your dad would've painted you, if he could've?

Maybe all I've learned is that the points of me don't always connect, but at least there's a glimmer of something—a vision of who I can become. With Theo, and Harper. With Mom, and with Dad. Our orbits are falling back into place, and I've found my own center, with my own gravitational pull.

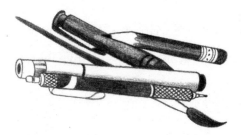

CHAPTER
twenty-eight

Over a month later, at the end of March, spring is here, and green is starting to bud around the city.

Harper announces that she wants to organize another charity card sale and asks me to make designs again. I'm looking forward to it this time. I know I can do it.

I sit with Harper and the Mermaids at lunch. And Theo's with us, too, now. He's also found his place, and realizes it's not so bad to have a little more sun on us.

There's another super moon. The Worm Moon.

It's called that because it marks the start of spring, when the earthworms emerge. Spring, the official time of new beginnings.

The day of the Full Worm Moon, the winners of NYC ART are announced.

Theo beams with happiness when Mr. Butterweit tells him that his Theo-Dare self-portrait has gotten in: one of ten selected out of all the New York City sixth-graders who entered the competition.

I, of course, am neither winner nor loser. I feel happiness for Theo's success, a twinge of sadness for myself, and a strong ray of hope. Hope that I can find my way forward.

To celebrate, Theo and I go to Golden Leaf Stationers for new art supplies.

Fareed smiles to see us there together again. I haven't been there since I bought the supplies for my lunar dust portrait. "Your mom settled the account," he whispers to me while Theo goes to town filling a shopping basket. "Anything else you need today?"

Theo's rich with the thousand-dollar reward to use, and so he treats me to a new set of tempera paints and three pads of watercolor sketch paper. Plus, surprise, my own lucky eraser, but in the shape of a dog.

There's nothing else I need for now, but I tell Fareed about the opening of the Hank Rosenbloom exhibition and invite him to come.

Evelyn Capstone was beside herself when I explained the whole situation to her. Actually, Mom and me. We met for lunch in the Petrie Sculpture Court. I told Evelyn what happened with G, *age 10*—what I discovered, what Theo did, and why I needed to get it back. She checked the backs of the canvases, and they all have the charcoal marks that correspond to the points on the drawings.

Now the asterism drawings are at the Met, where they'll be framed to hang in the Hank Rosenbloom exhibition. Along with *G in Blue*, the triangle portrait of me. It's weird that portraits of me are going to be hanging in the Met. Upstairs, in a real exhibition gallery. Not downstairs, in the education center, with all the student winners of NYC ART.

Before we know it, it's April, and time for the opening of both exhibitions.

NYC ART comes first. Mr. B and Mom and I are there, with Harriet, to help Theo celebrate on opening night. We even sneak in Krypto, in his tiny mesh carrier bag. Theo's entry looks amazing on the wall of the Met. And original: the only winning entry that's in comic form. Theo beams with pride, and I have just the tiniest pinch of jealousy that my work's not up there with his. But no one mentions anything about me—it's Theo's night, not mine.

The night of the opening of Dad's show, I realize that I feel different walking into the Met than I did the last few times I was there: at one with myself, in a way I wasn't before.

Which is good, because tonight, Mom and I are sort of the stars of the show. And Dad, of course, too. There's a giant banner hanging outside the building with the image of *Sally in the Stars* blown up and the name of the exhibition in large, bold letters: *Hank Rosenbloom: Artist and Man*.

And I think how he was—*is*—both.

Evelyn Capstone and Jenna are there. Along with Mr. B and Fareed. And Mrs. Velandry, supported by Theo and Harriet. Harper and her parents come as contributors to the exhibition, and also, as friends.

It's like a giant party to celebrate us. Our family.

A true memorial for Dad. Here we are, keeping him alive, in the present.

Journalists from all the big newspapers and art journals come to cover the opening: the *New York Times*, the *Wall Street Journal*, *ARTNews*. They want to take pictures of Mom and me posing together at the entrance of the show. There's a big empty hole next to me, on my other side, where Dad should be, where I'll always feel him missing. I shiver.

Then we turn around to walk into the first room,

and it's like he's here with us. I smile at Mom, and she squeezes my hand.

The first gallery is about Dad's early years, from elementary school, when his artistic talent first started to get recognized by his art teacher, to his college days, when he turned away from art, to advertising. To after college, when he was miserable working a desk job at an ad agency, and spent his nights painting.

Each room that follows shows the next decade of his life, his work, his career. In his forties, Mom and I come into the picture. Mom first, of course, but not by much. I was born four months after they were married.

We go from that room (which has walls painted in a bright white, *G in Blue* glowing to great effect), when Dad was reaching the height of his career and his personal life, into the dimness of what I know is the last, small room. The one just before the gift shop. The one where the asterism paintings and sketches hang.

It takes a second for my eyes to adjust. It's almost like a shrine in here, how Dad wanted it to be. The lights are low, the walls painted an ice blue.

The paintings pop against the light background, and I block out the murmurs of the people around me and let myself get absorbed in the canvases. Those paintings, hanging all together, for now.

And then, there are the drawings. The asterism sketches. Each one is in a freestanding, double-sided case, so you can see the front and back of the paper. How Dad drew an image and then sketched the points of the asterism on the back.

I read the label for *G, age 10*: "Rosenbloom's portrait of his daughter, Georgia, when she was ten years old, comes from one of his personal portfolios solely devoted to drawings of Georgia, from the time she was a baby until she was ten, just before he died.

"In this portrait of Georgia, we see her reading in a chair at home, eyes looking down, unaware of being drawn by her father.

"On the reverse, we see the pencil points, ten in total, perhaps one for each year of Georgia's life, that indicate that Rosenbloom intended to use this drawing as the model for his last asterism painting, which he never made."

I look at the three other asterism sketches: Mom, Dad, the bird.

But then, near the exit, my eyes widen in surprise. There's another framed image on the wall. A self-portrait.

My self-portrait. *Georgia in Orbit.*

Even I have to admit that it looks beautiful.

Mom had told me she was going to have it framed, but I had no idea she was putting it up in Dad's exhibition.

At the Met, no less.

It looks perfect.

Through the tears in my eyes, I read the label: *"Rosenbloom died before he could paint the last asterism. Over the years, there's been speculation as to what the subject might've been. Recently, with the recovery of the drawing* G, age 10 *and the recognition of the asterism points on the back by Georgia Rosenbloom, it was determined that she would've been the subject of the last asterism.*

"*Here is Georgia's own interpretation: a self-portrait drawn freehand in graphite. For the background, she used the same black paints that Rosenbloom used for his asterism paintings. The placement and number (twelve) and colors of the asterism points, done in tempera paint on tracing paper, laid onto the panel, are entirely her own.*"

"Wow," Theo says, coming up next to me. "That's yours, isn't it?" He looks from me to the portrait and back again.

"Yes," I say. "It's mine."

And ours.

Acknowledgments

There are many people to whom I give my thanks. First, my agent, Sara Crowe, for her belief in me and in Georgia, and to Pippin Properties. To my editor, Martha Mihalick, and the Greenwillow/ HarperCollins team for bringing this book into the world with such care. And to Vesper Stamper, for her stunning art.

I was fortunate to learn about the world of children's book publishing from two talented and generous mentors, Christy Ottaviano and Wendy Lamb.

Over many years of work and study, my writing grew from the feedback of teachers and guides at various stages: Mary Gordon, Uma Krishnaswami, Amy Hest, Sarah Aronson, Rebecca Petruck, Lisa Cron, and Julie Scheina. Sarah Mlynowski took me under her wing to show me what discipline means for a working writer. I'm not sure that I would've stuck to it without Julie Sternberg, Alyssa Sheinmel, and Jacqueline Resnick.

Tremendous thanks to the Metropolitan Museum of Art, where I have the privilege of presenting world-class art to the public and the friendship of my colleagues at the Volunteer Organization. Also, great appreciation for the New York Society Library, which provided me with a writing home for hours of work.

I'm grateful to my parents for supporting my childhood dream: my mother nourished my love of reading, and she taught me how to write by editing my work. My father read to me every night, and gave me the joy of "publishing" my first book.

Deepest thanks to my grandmothers and role models, Lola Finkelstein and the late Lillian Meckler; I hope their strength lives on in me. And to all the friends and family who've cheered and encouraged me.

Above all, never-ending love and gratitude for my chosen family: Jamie, who supports and stands by me; Dash, in his Shih Tzu glory; and Julia and Elizabeth, ideal readers, daughters of my dreams.